∾

Looking at her right hand, she was stunned to realize she held the crystal sword.

"If he could've lasted, maybe he would've won. But I lasted. I usually do," Alanna added bitterly. "I'm sorry I brought trouble to you." She started to turn away.

"One moment." Halef's voice was kind but firm. She looked back to see him pointing at the shaman's tent. "This is your home now."

Alanna braced her free hand on Kourrem's shoulder. "I don't understand."

Ali Mukhtab rose to stand beside the headman. "Halef Seif is right. You have slain the old shaman. You must now take his place until you teach a new shaman, or until one slays you."

It was too much. "That's crazy!" Alanna shouted, her voice cracking with weariness. "I'm not—I'm a knight! I've never taught sorcery—"

"Would you leave us defenseless against the shamans of the hillmen?" Halef asked quietly. Alanna closed her mouth, remembering the Bazhir tales of the hill-sorcerers. "That is the law. That is our custom." He opened the door flap of the shaman's tent. "This is your home now, Woman Who Rides Like a Man."

Song of the Lioness Quartet
By Tamora Pierce

Alanna: The First Adventure (Book One)

In the Hand of the Goddess (Book Two)

The Woman Who Rides Like a Man (Book Three)

Lioness Rampant (Book Four)

❧

And keep an eye out for Tamora Pierce's new Tortall series:

THE IMMORTALS

available for the first time in paperback,
from Random House Fantasy in May 1997:

Wild Magic (Book One)

Wolf-Speaker (Book Two)

Emperor Mage (Book Three)

The Woman Who Rides Like a Man

Song of the Lioness
Book Three

TAMORA PIERCE

Random House 🏠 New York

Library of Congress Catalog Card Number: 83-20054
ISBN: 0-679-80112-X
RL: 6.3

Printed in the United States of America 10

To Pa, Ma, and Kim—
my own personal pride of lions—
and particularly to Pa, who started
me writing in the first place

Contents

1. The Woman Who Rides Like a Man   1

2. The Bloody Hawk   22

3. Bazhir Shaman   45

4. Studies in Sorcery   67

5. Apprentices   85

6. Ceremonies   109

7. The Voice of the Tribes   142

8. The King of the Thieves   165

9. At the Sign of the Dancing Dove   190

10. The Doomed Sorceress   210

The Woman Who
Rides Like a Man

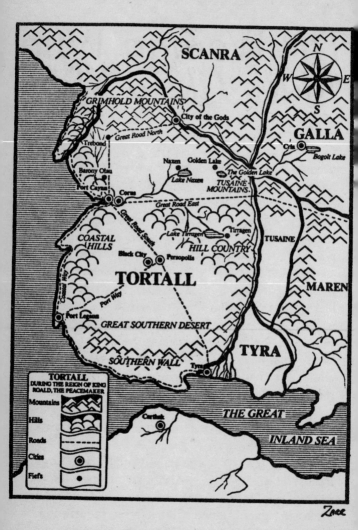

one

The Woman Who Rides Like a Man

𝒜lanna of Trebond, the sole woman knight in the realm of Tortall, splashed happily in the waters of an oasis, enjoying her first bath in three days. *Hard to believe that it's winter in the North,* she reflected. In the Southern Desert the temperatures were just right, although she objected to so much sand.

"Best hurry up," Coram told her. Her burly man-at-arms stood guard on the other side of the bushes that concealed the pool. "If this is a Bazhir waterin' place, we don't want to wait and find out if they swear for the King or against him."

Alanna stepped out of the water, grabbing her clothes. She had no urge to meet any Bazhir tribesmen, particularly not renegades. She and Coram were bound for Tyra in the south, and coming to battle with the warlike desert men would cut their journey very short.

Drying off, the young knight pulled on a boy's blue shirt and breeches. Although her femininity was not the secret it had been when she trained in the royal palace, Alanna still preferred the freedom of men's clothing. It was odd to remember that the last time she bathed in an oasis, she had been a page and Prince Jonathan had just found out she was girl. Those days—the days in which she bound her chest flat and never went swimming—were gone. She didn't miss them.

Faithful, her pet cat, was yowling a warning. "Alanna!" Coram yelled, seconding the cat. "We've got trouble!"

Grabbing her sword, Alanna raced for Coram and the horses. An approaching cloud of dust indicated tribesmen or robbers, and she grimaced as she threw herself into Moonlight's saddle. She trotted forward to meet Faithful, a small black streak racing toward her across the sand. The cat leaped, landing squarely in front of his mistress before climbing into the leather cup that was his position on her saddle. Alanna's gentle mare held steady, used to the cat's abrupt comings and goings.

"Let's try to reach the road!" Alanna told Coram.

They rode hard, Alanna crouched low over Moonlight's pale mane. She looked back to see Coram shaking his head. "It's no good," he was bellowing. "They've spotted us! Ride on—I'll hold 'em!"

Alanna wheeled and stopped, Lightning glittering in her hand. "What sort of friend d'you think I am? We'll wait for them here."

Coram swore. "If ye were my daughter, I'd tan yer hide! Go!"

Alanna shook her head stubbornly. She could see their pursuers now: they were hillmen, the worst of the desert raiders. Reaching behind her, she unbuckled her shield from its straps, slipping it over her left arm. Coram was following suit.

"Stubborn lass," he grumbled. "I'd druther tangle with ten Bazhir tribes than any hillmen."

Alanna nodded. The Bazhir were deadly fighters, but they had a strict code of honor. Hillmen lived for killing and loot.

Renewing her grip on Lightning's hilt, she settled her shield more firmly on her arm. The hillmen closed rapidly, fanning out in a half circle that would close around Alanna and her companion. Grimly the knight clenched her jaw and ordered, "Take them in a charge."

"*What?*" yelped Coram.

Alanna charged directly at the hillmen. Coram gulped and followed her, letting out a war cry.

Moonlight reared as they reached the first raiders, striking out with hooves: she had been trained for battle years ago. Alanna slashed about her with Lightning, ignoring her enemies' yells of fury.

A one-eyed villain closed in, grabbing her sword arm. With an angry yowl Faithful leaped from his cup with his claws unsheathed. The one-eyed hillman screamed and released Alanna, trying to pull the hissing cat away from his face.

"Lass! Beware!" Coram bellowed, trying to fend off three at once. He yelled in pain as one of them opened a deep gash on his sword arm. He swore and attacked again, dropping his shield and switching his sword to his good left hand.

Warned by her companion, Alanna whirled to face a giant hillman, a grinning mountain with red hair and long braided mustaches. He guided his shaggy pony with his knees, leaving his hands free to grip the hilt of a sword with an odd crystal blade. Alanna eyed its razor-sharp length and gulped, ducking beneath the redheaded man's first swing. He reversed it, and she blocked it with her shield just in time, yelping at the pain of impact. She struck back with Lightning, only to miss as her attacker darted away.

She refused to follow and fight on his terms. Instead she brought her lioness shield up and waited.

The giant returned, circling her carefully. His pony lunged forward, and Moonlight reared, warning it back with her flailing hooves. Alanna caught another blow from the crystal blade on her shield, feeling the shock through her entire body.

I hope my brother put plenty of magic on this shield, she thought grimly. *Otherwise it won't last through its first battle!*

She turned Moonlight as the giant circled her on his nimble pony. With a kick of her heels she urged the gold mare forward, slashing at her opponent. She was a knight of Tortall, and not to be toyed with!

She used every chance to break through his guard. He blocked her time after time, grinning infuriatingly.

Alanna drew back, breathing hard and fighting to keep her control. Now the giant returned the attack, and she blinked sweat from her eyes: she could not afford to make a mistake now! His tactics were different from those of the mounted knights she had fought before; she didn't know what to expect.

Suddenly the midday sun was directly in her eyes—he had maneuvered her just for this. Only at the last second did she glimpse his sword descending on her. She brought Lightning up hard, slamming her blade hilt-to-hilt with the giant's sword. There was a ring of clashing metal, and the downward sweep of the crystal edge was stopped.

Then Lightning broke, sheared off near the hilt.

Moonlight darted away, taking Alanna out of the hillman's range. Her mistress stared at the hilt she still gripped. Lightning had been her sword ever since she had been considered fit to carry one. How could she fight without it in her hand?

Coming out of her daze, Alanna fumbled for her axe. She was trembling with rage; it took all her self-control to keep from losing her temper completely and making a fatal mistake. Axe in hand, she charged the hillman with a yell. She didn't hear the warning cries of the other hillmen, or Coram's gleeful whoop; she heard only the wheezing of the giant's pony and her own choked breath. She swung, swearing as the hillman ducked and pulled out of her range. She was closing with him again when he yelled, seeing something behind her. To her fury, he whirled his pony and fled, calling to the few men he had left. Alanna spurred after him.

"Come back, coward!" she cried.

The giant turned to laugh and shake his sword at her. His voice was choked off as a black arrow sprouted in his chest. More arrows struck down the hillmen; only two escaped. They rode for all they were worth, pursued by five white-robed tribesmen.

A Bazhir, his white burnoose tied with a scarlet cord, rode toward Alanna as she dismounted. She was staring at the body of the hillman who had wielded the crystal sword. The blade lay beside him, gleaming against the sand. It glimmered and suddenly flashed, blinding her for a short moment. Alanna stared: against the yellow-orange fire that filled her sight was a picture.

A dark finger—or was it a pole?—pointed at a crystal-blue sky. Before it stood a man wearing tattered gray; his eyes were mad. She could smell wood smoke.

Her eyes cleared, and the vision was gone.

Reaching under her shirt, Alanna drew forth the token given to her by the Great Mother Goddess three years before. It had once been a coal in her campfire; now it was covered in clear stone, its fires still flickering under its surface. Alanna knew that if she held it when magic was present, she could see power as a glowing force in the air. She saw magic now as orange light flickered around the sword, and she scowled. Recently she had dealt with magic of this particular shade, and the memory was not pleasant.

The Bazhir who had followed her kicked sand over the sword. "It is evil," he said, his quiet voice slightly raspy. "Let the desert have it."

Distracted from the magic, Alanna discovered she was crying. It was as if she had lost a companion, not a weapon.

A glint of metal caught her eye and she stopped to pick up Lightning's sheared-off blade. Sliding the length of metal into its sheath, she strapped the now-useless hilt in place. Unless she tried to draw the blade, no one would know it was not whole.

Mounting her horse, she settled Faithful before her as Coram brought his gelding to her side. "I'm sorry, lass," he told her quietly, putting a hand on her arm. "I know what the sword meant to ye. But ye can't be thinking of that now. These men may be friends or may not be; who knows why they saved our skins. Ye'd best be puttin' yer mind to talk with 'em."

Alanna nodded, trying to collect her thoughts. Their rescuers formed a loose circle around her and Coram as the man who had covered the crystal sword with sand joined them, guiding a large chestnut stallion with ease. The others gave way to him, letting him approach Alanna and Coram. For a while he said nothing, only stared.

Finally he nodded. "I am Halef Seif, headman of the Bloody Hawk tribe, of the people called the Bazhir," he said formally. "Those who are dead were trespassers on our sands, riding without leave. You also come here unbidden. Why should we not serve you as we did these others, Woman Who Rides Like a Man?"

Alanna rubbed her head tiredly. She felt too tired and dazed for the dance of manners that passed for conversation among the Bazhir. Dealing with these desert warriors was bound to be tricky; luckily she had learned their ways from an expert.

Faithful climbed onto her shoulder, setting up a murmur among the watching tribesmen. Alanna glared up at the cat, knowing he knew he was making the Bazhir nervous. *They don't see black cats with purple eyes often,* she thought. "You're getting too big to sit up there," she whispered to her pet.

Never mind that, Faithful told her. His meowing had always made as much sense to Alanna as human speech. *Talk to them now.*

Suddenly she felt more confident and alert. "I hope you will deal with us fairly, Halef Seif of the Bloody Hawk," she replied. "We took nothing. We harmed nothing, my friend and I. We are simply riding south. Would you harm a warrior of the King?"

Her gamble failed as Halef Seif shrugged. "We know no king."

Alanna could hear Coram shifting nervously in his saddle. It might have been easier to deal with men who acknowledged King Roald of Tortall. Renegades would not take kindly to the presence of Roald's most unusual young knight.

"You know no king, but others of the Bazhir do. If they knew you held a Knight of the Realm and her companion, they might counsel you to take care," Alanna warned.

This produced some amusement among the riders. Only their leader remained grim. "Is your king so weak he uses women for warriors? We cannot think well of such a king. We cannot think well of a woman so immodest that she puts on the clothes of a man and rides with her face bare."

Alanna pointed to the bodies of the hillmen she and Coram had slain. "*They* did not think I was a worthy opponent either. Can you say that my friend and I would be dead at the hillmen's swords if you had not come? They took my sword from me." She swallowed hard and said recklessly, "What is a sword? I have my axe, and my dagger, and my spear. I have Coram Smythesson to watch my back, as I watch his."

"Big words from a small woman," Halef Seif remarked. There was no way for Alanna to read his expression.

One of the riders, a Bazhir head and shoulders taller than most of his companions, brought his horse forward, peering at Alanna's face intently. Suddenly he nodded with satisfaction. "She is the one!" he exclaimed. "Halef, she is the Burning-Brightly One!"

"Speak on, Gammal," Halef ordered.

The huge warrior was bowing as low to Alanna as his saddle would permit. "Would you remember me?" he asked hopefully. "I was at the smallest west gate in the stone village that northerners call Persopolis. It was six rainy seasons ago. Your master, the Blue-Eyed One, bought my silence with a gold coin."

Remembering, Alanna grinned. "Of course! And you spat on the coin and bit it."

The big man looked at his chief. "She is the one! She came with the Blue-Eyed Prince, the Night One, and they freed us from the Black City!" He made the Sign against Evil close to his chest. "I let them through the gate that morning!"

Halef frowned as he watched Alanna. "Is this so?"

Alanna shrugged. "Prince Jonathan and I went to the Black City, yes," she admitted. "And we fought with the Ysandir—the Nameless Ones," she said hurriedly as the men muttered uneasily. "And we beat them. It wasn't easy."

A skinny man wearing the green robes of a Bazhir shaman, or petty wizard, threw back his hood. His scraggly beard thrust forward on a sallow chin. "She lies!" he cried, putting his horse between

Alanna and the tribesmen. "The Burning-Brightly One and the Night One rode into the sky in a chariot of fire when the Nameless Ones perished. This all men know!"

"They rode back to the stone village, on horses," Gammal replied stubbornly. "And the mare ridden by the Burning-Brightly One was even as this one now—the color of sand, with a mane and tail like the clouds."

While the Bazhir argued among themselves, Coram drew near his mistress. "Now what've ye gone an' done?" he asked softly.

"I think it's more a question of what Jon and I did," Alanna whispered back. "I told you about going to the Black City, didn't I? We fought demons there, and Jon found out I was really a girl. It was six years ago."

"If I'd known I'd be ridin' with a legend, I'd've thought twice about comin' along," Coram grumbled.

"Silence!" Halef ordered them all. He looked at Alanna. "For the moment, let us accept that you are a warrior of the Northern King, Woman Who Rides Like a Man. Your shield is proof of that. As headman of the Bloody Hawk, I invite you to share our fire this night."

Alanna eyed the tall Bazhir, wondering, *Do I have a choice?* Finally she bowed. "We are honored by your invitation. Certainly we could not think of refusing."

～

*T*he tent she and Coram were given to share was large and airy, well stocked with comfortable pillows and rugs. Alanna flopped down, thinking of what she had seen of the village itself. A rough count of the tents indicated the Bloody Hawk encompassed at least twenty families. Some of the bachelors would live apart from their parents in a single large tent. The shaman, the man wearing the burnoose tied with green cord, had vanished into the largest tent in the village; from what her teacher Sir Myles had taught her, his dwelling would double as the tribe's temple.

Her reverie was interrupted by three young members of the tribe. Two wore the face veil all Bazhir women put on when they began their women's cycles of monthly bleeding. The taller girl balanced a tray of food and wine. Carefully she placed it on the ground between Coram and Alanna as the other girl and a tall, handsome boy stared at the guests.

"We have never seen a woman with light eyes," the boy said abruptly. "Did the water that falls from the sky in the north wash all the color away?"

"Of course it didn't, Ishak," the smaller girl retorted. "How would her eyes be purple, then?"

"Ishak! Kourrem! Hush!" the girl who had carried the tray snapped. She bowed very low to Alanna and Coram. "Forgive my friends. They for-

get that they have been made adults of the tribe."
She glared at her friends. "I let you come with me
because you promised not to say anything. You
broke your word!"

"I didn't swear it by my ancestors," the boy
called Ishak said virtuously.

"Will your cat let me pet him?" Kourrem, the
smaller girl, asked Alanna. "His eyes are purple, too.
He is very handsome. Is he your brother, who was
turned into a cat by great sorcery?"

Faithful, looking smug over the praise, saun-
tered over to the visitors, letting them pet and
admire him. Alanna smiled at their guess that she
and Faithful were related somehow. Many others
had wondered about the fact that she and the cat
had the same eye color.

"No," she replied, pouring wine for Coram and
herself. "Faithful is just a cat. My brother is a sorcerer, but he is still shaped as a human—or he was
when I saw him last."

"I am Kara," the tall girl announced. "I am to
serve you until your fate is decided by the tribe.
And now we should go," she admitted reluctantly.
"We weren't supposed to stay long. Akhnan Ibn
Nazzir says you will corrupt us if we are not care-
ful."

Alanna and Coram exchanged worried glances.
"Who is this—" Coram made a face at his inability
to remember the harsh Bazhir name. "The one who
says we'll corrupt ye?"

"Akhnan Ibn Nazzir," Ishak said from the doorway. "The shaman, He says you are demons who have come to try our faith."

Kourrem crossed her eyes. "Ibn Nazzir is an old stick with a beard like weeds."

Shocked, Kara ushered Kourrem and Ishak from the tent. Coram shook his head worriedly. "I don't like the smell of this," he admitted. "D'ye think there's anything we can do?"

Alanna was rolling herself up in an embroidered throw. "*I* plan to take a nap." She yawned. "Until the tribe decides what to do with us, we can't do a thing." Within moments she was fast asleep, Faithful curled up beside her nose.

Coram was working on his third cup of date wine when Halef Seif looked into the tent. "She looks softer when she sleeps," he commented quietly. "When she awakes, tell her the tribe will decide your fate before the evening meal, at the campfire. I will send for you."

Coram nodded and finished his wine. Alanna was right; there was little they could do now. Making himself comfortable, he took a nap of his own.

⮊

The last streaks of sunlight were fading in the west when Alanna woke from her nap. Coram was still asleep, snoring lightly, and Faithful had vanished. Yawning and stretching, she stepped outside to find the village oddly still, as if it had been deserted. She would have gone to explore when Ishak—who was crouched beside the doorway of her tent—caught at her pant leg. Covering his lips with a warning finger, he led her back into the tent.

"It is the Moment of the Voice," he explained when they were inside. Coram was smoothing his sleep-ruffled hair. "All adults in the tribe must be present, but I was told to attend you." He looked up as voices sounded outside. "It is over, and soon they will call you. I will take you to them."

"Aren't ye afraid we'll corrupt ye?" Coram asked kindly.

The boy shook his head. "Halef Seif says only the man who wishes to be corrupted will fall into evil ways. Halef Seif is wise in the ways of men."

"Wiser than your shaman?" Alanna asked.

"Akhnan Ibn Nazzir is an old desert hen," the boy said scornfully. "His magic hurts more than it helps." He looked eagerly at Alanna. "Ibn Nazzir says you are a sorceress from the North. Will you teach me your sorcery? Look! Already I know a little!" Reaching out, he concentrated on the ball of reddish fire growing at his fingertips.

Alanna knocked his hand away, breaking Ishak's concentration. "I know nothing of magic," she said harshly. "And I want to know nothing of magic. The Gift only leads to pain and death."

Kara peered in the doorway and bowed. "Ishak, help our guests to get ready," she commanded. She swallowed hard, looking at Alanna. "Will you need help, Woman Who Rides Like a Man?"

Alanna smiled. "Thank you, Kara, I can manage for myself."

The girl bowed again. "Ishak will bring you to the central fire when you are ready," she said before letting the tent flap fall.

Coram was already breaking open one of Alanna's saddlebags, bringing out her mail shirt and leggings. Ishak gasped with admiration, touching the gold-washed armor with reverent fingers. Alanna had been given the mail by her friends on her eighteenth birthday. Although she had plain steel mail to wear, this was specially made for her and particularly light. She fastened the amethyst-trimmed belt at her waist, removing the sheaths for sword and dagger. It would not be polite to go armed, and it still hurt to look at Lightning. She hooked gauntlets decorated with her lioness rampant design into her belt and nodded to Coram. "I'll wait for you two outside," she said casually. "I need to think."

She was actually responding to Faithful's soft hiss just outside the tent. She went to stand beside her pet, scanning the rapidly falling darkness. "What do you want?" she whispered. "We have these people to—"

Shadows moved against the night, and she froze. Akhnan Ibn Nazzir was leading a horse into the darkness. "Now, what do you suppose he's up to?" Alanna asked Faithful. "D'you think he means trouble for us?"

Yes, the cat replied. *He was asking the young ones who came into your tent what you had of value. I don't think he asked because he means well.*

Alanna sighed and followed Ishak and Coram to the campfire. Wasn't life difficult enough without earning the enmity of a Bazhir shaman?

She was given the place on Halef Seif's right, with Coram beside her and Faithful settling down in front of her crossed legs. As the men of the tribe settled into the great circle formed by the firelight, Alanna took a closer look at Halef Seif. With his burnoose off his head, the headman looked to be in his late thirties. He was hook-nosed and lean; sharp lines were drawn from his nostrils to the corners of his thin mouth. *A man who's seen a lot of life,* Alanna decided.

The women of the tribe watched from behind the men, their eyes glittering over their face veils. Alanna tried to keep her nervousness hidden; she wanted to make friends of these people, and she had no way of knowing if they wanted to make a friend of her. A flicker of green caught her attention, and she turned with the others to watch the shaman take his place opposite Halef Seif. He looked pleased with himself. Something told Alanna he had been up to mischief.

Halef raised his voice so everyone could hear. "There are two voices in our tribe. One speaks for the acceptance of the intruders, saying they are a sacred one and the servant of a sacred one, deserving honor at our hands. One calls for their deaths, saying they are the servants of the King in the North, and that women must not act as men. By our custom, the strangers must hear each voice and answer. So it has always been. Before others speak, I will say what I must say. I am headman of the Bloody Hawk: this is my right.

"I do not know that this woman is the Burning-Brightly One who came with the Night One to free us from the Black City. She claims to serve the King in the North, and he is our enemy. Yet she came here in peace until the hillmen attacked her. Then she fought well. She and her servant killed many of the hillmen, who are our foes.

"She rides as a man, goes unveiled as a man, fights as a man. Let her prove herself worthy as a man, worthy of her weapons and of our friendship." Finished, he bowed his dark head.

The arguing began, with the shaman speaking next. Alanna wasn't surprised to hear him accuse her of blasphemy against the gods for her manner of dress and her way of life—some of the priests at the royal palace had said much the same, when her true identity had been revealed. Gammal followed the shaman, once again telling the story of the strange events at the Black City, six years before.

One tall Bazhir named Hakim Fahrar spoke of
the penalty owed to any outsiders: death. And others in the tribe asked for moderation, saying that
people who did not change with new times were
doomed to extinction. The debate went on and on
while Faithful took a nap. If her life and Coram's
had not been at stake, Alanna would have been
bored by the long speeches. As it was, she felt a
growing respect for Halef Seif's insistence on hearing each man's opinion. It was not the first time she
noticed the great concern the Bazhir people had for
the right of all to speak out (in some matters even
the women had a say, she discovered later), but it
would not be the last.

Only once did they say something to puzzle
her. "The Voice gave her and the Blue-Eyed Prince
honor when they returned from battle with
the Nameless Ones," Gammal told the shaman
hotly.

"The Voice also says we must decide her fate
ourselves, Gammal," Halef warned. "Be still. Justice
will be done."

Alanna frowned. Ishak had mentioned a
"Moment of the Voice," now Gammal and the
headman spoke of "The Voice." *Did Myles ever tell
me of a Bazhir god or priest by that name?* she wondered. *I don't think so. I'll ask Halef Seif about his
"Voice"—if I survive the night.*

The oldest man of the tribe raised his hand.
"There is a way to decide this woman's status. She

bears weapons as a man—let her fight as a man. Give her the trial by combat. If she wins, the tribe is wise to accept her. If she loses, let her servant be killed also."

The shaman jumped up, screaming, "The favor of the gods to the man who kills her! I swear it!"

"If the favor of the gods is offered," Alanna asked mildly, "why don't you kill me yourself?" There was a murmur of laughter, and the shaman whirled to glare at Alanna.

"She mocks our ways!" he cried.

"I mock a shaman who looks at the goods I possess and calls for my death because he says I offend the gods. Can you tell me you have no interest in what I own?" she asked steadily, her eyes never wavering from his staring ones.

Halef rubbed his chin thoughtfully. "One third of what you have goes to him who slays you. One third goes to the headman. One third goes to the priest. It has always been so."

Alanna smiled angrily. "I thought as much."

Halef Seif raised his hands. "The men of the tribe will vote on this matter: to grant the Woman Who Rides Like a Man the trial by combat."

Women passed among the men with bits of parchment, reeds for writing, and ink. They returned to collect the folded papers, and Halef Seif counted them. He took great care to unfold each paper and place it in one of two piles before him, so that no one could accuse him of manipulating the vote. Once again Alanna was impressed with Bazhir honesty.

At last the votes were counted. "It is the combat," Halef Seif announced.

two

The Bloody Hawk

*A*lanna stood, nervously rubbing her suddenly wet palms on her tunic. "I accept the will of the tribe. Who will carry it out?"

Hakim Fahrar stood. "The law is the law. I will fight for the tribe."

Alanna bent to strip away her boots and stockings, examining her would-be opponent. He was head and shoulders taller than she, and his naked torso showed hard muscles in the firelight. He seemed agile enough, but only the fight would confirm that.

Coram tied her hair back with a leather thong, his callused hands gentle. As she began her loosening-up exercises, he knelt beside her. "Be careful," he cautioned, his voice a whisper. "They fight to the death here."

Alanna scrubbed her palms with sand to dry them. "I won't kill if I don't have to," she replied quietly, remembering her last duel.

Coram shrugged. "Be that as it may, if it's a question of ye dyin' or him, it had better be him."

Alanna grinned mischievously at her longtime

teacher and accepted her dagger from Ishak, who had brought it from her tent. "I won't argue with that."

She waited for the shaman to finish exhorting her opponent, fingering the ember-stone. There was no way she could avoid remembering her duel four weeks ago, the one that had ended with Duke Roger on the floor of the Great Hall, dead. Unlike the sorcerer-duke, she did not hate this tribesman. She hoped it would not come to killing tonight.

Halef stood. "Are you ready, man of the tribe?"

Hakim saluted the headman with his dagger. "I am ready."

"Are you ready, Woman of the Northern King?"

Alanna saluted, her mouth paper-dry. "I am."

The headman clapped his hands sharply and the tribesmen stepped back. Hakim circled, his eyes sharp.

"Meet your death, woman!" he cried.

Alanna crouched, watching his circling form and remaining silent. She had never followed the practice of shouting insults at an enemy; this was no time to start. Remembering the advice of her friend George, the King of the Thieves, she kept her eyes on Hakim's blade. He thrust; she skipped aside, then danced in close, slashing for his chest. He leaped back and began to circle once more, his eyes wary. Her lightning response had taught him to treat her with caution.

He feinted high and then drove in, his knife

coming up from beneath. Alanna turned her side toward him; as his arm shot past her, she seized it and wrenched him over her hip. Coram let out a whoop of joy—wrestling had always been her weak point—and silenced himself as the Bazhir glared at him.

Hakim rolled to his feet as she kept back, unwilling to follow up her advantage. He wiped his hands on his breeches, his eyes never leaving her. He was sweating, and Alanna could feel the fear rolling off him. *Teach him to think a woman's an easy opponent,* she thought as she lunged in.

He caught her cross guard on his, bearing up on the locked knives. Alanna dropped and rolled away before coming to her feet. Hakim lunged wildly, his blade slicing toward her unprotected shoulder. Twisting, Alanna stabbed through the web of muscle on the bottom of his upper arm. She yanked her knife free just as one of his fists struck the middle of her spine, driving the wind from her lungs. Again she dropped and rolled. He threw himself toward her: this time she helped him over her head with her foot, sending him flying across the cleared space.

Breathing hard, she rolled to her feet. Hakim rose, dashing sweat from his eyes. He closed too slowly, giving her time to maneuver into position. Grabbing his knife arm, she rapped him hard on the temple with her dagger hilt. Hakim went down like a stone, and stayed down.

"You may kill him," Halef told her. "It is your right."

Alanna wiped her sweating face. "I won't kill when I don't have to. I hate waste."

Men assisted Hakim from the circle as Coram gave her a towel. Faithful twined around her ankles. "Ye did well," the ex-soldier whispered. "Any of us who taught ye would've been proud of that fight."

The Bazhir crowded around to offer their congratulations. Only a few stayed back, including the shaman, Akhnan Ibn Nazzir. Thinking to make amends, Alanna went to him, her hand outstretched. "Is there peace between us?" she asked. "I mean no offense to you or your ways."

"Unnatural woman!" he snarled. "The Balance will never be right as long as you act like a man!" He glared at the now-silent Bazhir. "Our tribe will suffer until this she-demon is cast out!" Gathering his burnoose around himself, he stalked off.

For a moment all were silent. Finally Alanna shrugged and turned to Halef Seif.

"Now what?" she asked.

The headman's set face boded ill for the shaman. Then he too shrugged. "The law is the law. You survived the combat: you are one of us." The tribesmen murmured their agreement. "Akhnan Ibn Nazzir is no longer young. New ideas come less easily to him." He smiled at her. "Now we make you a warrior of the tribe, and your man Coram, if you will speak for him."

"Of course I'll speak for him." How could he ask?

"Then hold out your arm," Halef instructed. Alanna obeyed. In a swift movement the man opened a long shallow cut on the inside of her forearm. Holding out his own wrist, he did the same to himself, then pressed his wound to Alanna's.

"Become one with the tribe, and one with our people," he commanded, his soft voice suddenly deep and ringing. Alanna shuddered as an alien magic flooded into her body. She knew without being told that Halef Seif was only a pathway for this sorcery, that its origins were as old as the Bazhir tribes.

Their combined blood welled up, dripping onto the sand. The watching men set up a cheer. Touching the ember-stone, she watched as Gammal performed the ritual with Coram. The magic was glittering white; it filled the air around them all, flooding from every Bazhir present.

She let Ishak bind up her arm, feeling a moment's sympathy for Coram. The ex-soldier was obviously unhappy that he had taken part in an exercise of sorcery (albeit a short one). Now they were truly members of the Bazhir, tied by blood and magic to the desertmen.

The drinking started. Women brought out food as the men told stories, recounting their greatest legends for the two new members of the tribe. The sky was gray in the east when Alanna gave up and went to bed. Coram had been moved into bachelor quarters; evidently her new status did not excuse her from the proprieties. Amused, she fell onto her pillow and sank immediately into sleep.

Sunlight in her eyes roused her. Her tent flap was open; from the sun's position she saw it was noon. Moaning and clutching her aching head, Alanna lurched to her feet.

"We've been waiting forever," Kourrem announced.

Alanna scowled at the two Bazhir girls who had welcomed her the previous day. "I didn't go to bed till dawn," she growled. She ducked behind a partition and changed her clothes, feeling very old and much the worse for a night of date wine.

"They made you a warrior of the tribe." Kara's voice was filled with awe. "And you're a woman."

Alanna pulled on the fresh tan burnoose she found with her clothes. If she was a Bazhir, she might as well dress like one. Emerging from behind the partition, she bathed her face in a basin of water.

"Akhnan Ibn Nazzir says you're a demon," Kourrem told her. "He says you have destroyed the eternal Balance. He wants us all to kill you."

Alanna dried her face briskly and pulled a comb through her hair before answering. "Nonsense. If your eternal Balance is destroyed, why did the sun rise? If I'm a demon, why do I have such a headache?" Using fresh water, she cleaned her teeth.

"Are all the women in the North warriors?" Kourrem asked. Kara was setting out breakfast: fruit and chilled fruit juice, rolls and cheese. "Are you all sorcerers and she-demons?"

Alanna rubbed her aching head. Was she supposed to eat all that? "Hardly," she replied to Kourrem. She sat awkwardly before the low table, crossing her legs before her. Inspired, she told the girls, "Why don't you join me? I'd welcome the company." It wasn't quite the truth, but chances were the girls would be far hungrier than she was at the moment.

Kourrem needed no urging, but Kara hesitated. "It wouldn't be proper," she demurred, her eyes uncertain over her face veil.

"Of course it's proper," Alanna said firmly. "I'm female, aren't I? At least, I was the last time I checked."

Even Kara smiled at that. She and Kourrem slipped off their veils. Kara was older, fine-boned and dark-eyed, with two deep-set dimples framing her mouth. Kourrem had mischievous gray-brown eyes and a pointed little chin. Both were too thin, even for rapidly growing teenagers, and their clothes were of poor quality. If Alanna remembered Sir Myles's teaching correctly, both were old enough to be married; the desert people contracted alliances for their daughters when they first donned veils, at the age of twelve. Why were these two single?

Alanna picked up a roll, and the girls eagerly helped themselves.

"If the Northern women aren't warriors," Kourrem went on, her mouth full, "how did *you* become a knight?"

Alanna smiled reluctantly. "It wasn't easy," she admitted. Seeing that her audience was listening intently, she sighed. "I was ten. My mother died giving my twin brother and me birth, and our father was a scholar who cared more for his work than us. Coram raised us, and old Maude, who was our village healing-woman. You see, Thom had no turn for woodcraft and archery, and I did. He was good at magical things.

"When our father decided it was time for me to go to the convent and learn to be a lady, I didn't want to. And Thom didn't want to go to the palace and become a knight."

"You changed places," whispered Kourrem. Kara's eyes were like saucers.

Alanna nodded. "Thom forged letters from our father. He went to the City of the Gods, and I went to the palace as his twin 'brother' Alan."

"Did your brother disguise himself as a girl?" Kara wanted to know.

Alanna laughed. "Of course not! The Daughters at the convent took boys who would be priests and sorcerers, until they were twelve or so. Then Thom went to the Mithran priests to complete his studies. He left them only a few months ago; he's the youngest Master living."

"He must have great power," Kara breathed.

"He certainly does," Alanna replied slowly. *And the ambition to go with it,* she added to herself.

"You lived as a boy all those years?" Kourrem demanded. "And no one guessed? No one knew?"

"One of my teachers, Sir Myles of Olau, guessed. I had to use magic to save Prince Jonathan when he had the Sweating Sickness, and Myles was watching; he must have seen something that gave me away. He knew for years, but he never told anyone. I told George Cooper when I needed a healing-woman once."

"Who is this George Cooper?" asked Kourrem.

Alanna grinned. "The King of the Thieves."

"You told a *thief* your secret?" Kara gasped.

"I knew I could trust him. He's always done well by me."

"Did anyone else know?" Kourrem's mouth was full again.

"Prince Jonathan found out, when we fought the Ysandir." Both girls made the Sign against Evil; like all Bazhir, they had grown up fearing the Ysandir. "They made my clothes disappear," Alanna continued, blushing. "By that time I was old enough—there was no way Jon could have misunderstood."

"Your chest," Kara nodded. Started, she added, "That's right! How did you manage disguising *that?*"

"I bound myself," Alanna confessed. "I never

took my shirt off around the boys, either. It was difficult at first, but after a while they just accepted the fact that I was eccentric."

"I still don't understand." Kara was frowning. "Women are weaker than men, and unfitted to be warriors. Surely they could tell——"

"Not from me," Alanna said firmly, finishing off her juice. "I worked hard to win my shield. I got up early; I practiced late at night. It was hard, very hard. But it was worth it. I was good enough that Jonathan made me his squire."

"Did he change his mind when he found out the truth?" Kourrem asked as she tidied up.

Alanna's blush returned. "No. He said he didn't care, I was still one of the best fighters at Court."

"None of *our* men would've said that," Kourrem muttered. "Even if it was true."

"You can't know that," Alanna told the younger girl. "I didn't find out until recently that Myles had known all these years. Men are peculiar." Looking at Kara, she said, "Why are you so unhappy?"

"You never had a young man," Kara explained mournfully. "You know—to bring you tokens, to take you walking——"

"Neither have we," Kourrem reminded her.

"We're practically outcasts from the tribe," Kara responded. "Surely Alanna's case is different."

"Unless Prince Jonathan——" Kourrem muttered. Both girls saw the misty smile on Alanna's face and giggled.

"It's time for me to have a look around the village," Alanna told them as she rose. She couldn't explain that her relationship with Jon had progressed far beyond the tokens-and-walks stage. Neither could she tell these two innocents that George, the King of the Thieves, had indicated more than once he would like to take Jonathan's place in her affections.

They would just be confused, Alanna told herself as the girls donned face veils once more. *Although they certainly can't be any more confused than I am.*

❧

The dust-colored tent village was quiet, except for the laughter of children and the cackle of chickens. Few men were visible; *either riding or sleeping off last night,* Alanna thought grumpily. Most of the women abroad hurried out of her path. Puzzled, she stopped to see if anyone would meet her eyes. Only the youngest children did, and they were snatched from her sight by their mothers.

"They really *do* think I'm some kind of demon," she whispered, shocked.

"They're just ignorant," Kourrem replied stubbornly. "*We* know—Kara and Ishak and I—that you're an ordinary woman."

"Not an *ordinary* woman," Kara demurred. "But you're *real*."

Alanna halted. "What makes you three so ready to believe I'm really human?" she asked. The girls exchanged looks.

"Akhnan Ibn Nazzir says the three of us are easily distracted from the right path, and that we are the growing-ground for evil," Kara explained. Her face had darkened. "Perhaps I *am* a growing-ground for evil!" she cried. "But I am not a mean old man who cannot countenance anything new! I don't make people outcasts because they don't bow down to me!"

Kourrem nodded solemnly. "It's true," she assured Alanna. "Halef Seif will not let him cast us out into the desert, but if Akhnan Ibn Nazzir is still here when Halef Seif dies—"

"Demon!"

The shriek of rage came from behind them. Alanna spun, her hand instantly going to Lightning's hilt. For a moment her heart twisted with pain as she remembered that her sword was useless.

Ibn Nazzir, the shaman, stood behind them, flanked by women and a few men. "Demon!" he screamed again, pointing a trembling finger at Alanna. "Not content with the soul of Halef Seif, you try to steal our young ones!" He grabbed Kara's arm and yanked, almost making her fall.

Halef Seif came out of a nearby tent, going to stand beside Alanna and Kourrem. He raised polite brows. "I believe I retain my soul, Akhnan Ibn Nazzir," he said quietly. "Surely I would know if it was gone."

Alanna stared wide-eyed at the sword, which

Ibn Nazzir had not been wearing the day before. It was the crystal sword that had so neatly sheared Lightning's blade, the sword she thought was left in the desert. *So that's what he was doing, sneaking off last night!* she thought. The sword's hilt design was distinctive; where had she seen it before?

"She has bewitched you!" the shaman cried, his eyes bulging with fury. "As she has bewitched these others—" The wave of his hand took in the girls. He gasped as Faithful suddenly leaped out, seemingly from nowhere, to land spitting in the sand before the shaman. "Away, demon!" he cried. Frantically he drew shimmering yellow magical symbols in the air.

Alanna reacted. "Stop!" A wall of purple magic streaked from her fingers to surround Faithful, just as yellow fire left the shaman's hands. It shattered against the wall protecting Faithful; Ibn Nazzir swore. For a moment there was silence as the violet wall faded from sight.

"Perhaps now you will give more courtesy to the companions of the Woman Who Rides Like a Man, Akhnan Ibn Nazzir," Halef Seif commented, his voice a quiet warning. "Tell me now where you obtained the sword you wear."

"It lay in the desert for anyone to take it who could," the older man spat. "I knew the spells to assuage its hunger and to give it greater life—"

"Let me see it," Halef Seif ordered, stretching out his hand. When the shaman hesitated, the younger man's face grew stern. "I am headman here, and headman I stay until the Voice of the Tribes takes my right from me. The request is reasonable. Do not defy me."

Trembling with fury, the shaman unclipped the sword's sheath and held it out. The headman reached for it.

Stop him! Faithful warned.

"Don't touch it!" Alanna cried.

Everyone looked at her. Ibn Nazzir glared pure hate. Fingering Lightning's hilt, Alanna continued.

"Such swords bite, Halef Seif. I imagine Akhnan Ibn Nazzir knows it, too." She gripped the silver hilt of the crystal blade and drew it.

The sword's magic screeched through her. Alanna bit back a yell of pain. Sweat poured down her face as she struggled with pure magic, forcing it slowly to her will.

At last the sword's resistance lessened. She looked up at Halef. "It might've killed you, unless you have the Gift." The man shook his head. "It's magic, but the magic's been used for killing and breaking. It can only be controlled by someone with the Gift. You don't have to be a great sorcerer—just stubborn."

Halef Seif rounded on Ibn Nazzir. "You knew this?" His soft voice was dangerous.

"I swear I did not!" the shaman cried. "I know of the power, as would any man who grasped it in his hand—"

"Or any woman," murmured Ishak, who had followed Halef.

Ibn Nazzir glared at him swiftly before returning to Halef Seif. "That it would harm, even kill, the headman—" He drew himself up as far as he could. "Such an offense is one no shaman would commit, Halef Seif. Has this woman so corrupted you that you see evil everywhere you turn?"

Alanna studied the crystal sword. Its hilt was slightly longer than Lightning's, etched with occult symbols and studded at the pommel with sapphires and diamonds. She had seen symbols like these recently....

Remembering, she dropped the blade, backing away from it in horror. The shaman stooped and grabbed it, slamming it into its sheath.

"What's wrong with ye?" Coram demanded softly. She had not seen him arrive.

"Roger," she whispered. "The hilt—it's the same as Duke Roger's wizard's rod! I'll never be free of him!" She turned and fled to her tent, Faithful galloping after her.

"Who is this 'Roger'?" Halef Seif asked Coram as the crowd dispersed.

Alanna's friend waited until they were alone before he replied, and he kept his powerful voice low. "Duke Roger of Conté. Him that was next in line to Prince Jonathan for the throne of Tortall."

Halef made the Sign against Evil. "The great sorcerer who was killed not one moon past?"

Coram nodded. "Aye. *She* slew him, for his plot to kill the Queen." He sighed. "She always hated the Duke, feared him, even. He felt the same about her. She killed him in proper combat, before the King and his Court, but she never felt right about it." His dark eyes were thoughtful. "I'd give a lot to know how a sword that looks like *his* wizard's rod turned up in her path now."

Halef Seif put his hand on Coram's shoulder. "She has been chosen by the gods. Is that not reason enough?"

∿

*A*lanna remained alone in her tent until dark, petting Faithful and remembering. No matter how she looked at it, she could see no way she could have done things differently. Made wary—and aware—by her Ordeal of Knighthood, she had searched Duke Roger's quarters. She had found enough evidence to damn him in any eyes: the wax model of the Queen, worn away by falling water until the Queen herself was close to death; wax images of the King, the Prince, and the important Court officials, even one of Alanna, all tied up in a thick veil. She had taken the evidence to King Roald, presented it before the entire Court. Roger had demanded a trial by combat: she had won.

She had hated Roger of Conté, but she couldn't forget the sight of him as he was carried into his tomb far beneath the palace. She'd spent so much of her life thinking about the sorcerer who was Jonathan's cousin that it was hard to realize he was gone.

You're being ridiculous, Faithful commented. *He would have cut you up and fed you to wild beasts if he had won. He was evil. He deserved to die.*

"I wish I could view it that simply," Alanna said ruefully. "I still wonder if perhaps I moved too fast."

That's what he wanted you to think. Remember? was the cat's tart reply.

Alanna shook her head, still unconvinced. "Merciful Mother, is it dark already?"

"Night comes swiftly here," Halef commented from the doorway. He crouched beside her, his face in shadow. "Already we have communed with the Voice of the Tribes. He comes."

"Who is this 'Voice of the Tribes'?" Alanna wanted to know.

"He is the first among us," the headman replied. "At sunset we gather at our fires and join with him—each man and woman among the Bazhir. Thus he knows our thoughts, our wishes. He knows what has passed during the day. He judges with complete knowledge of our hearts and our minds."

Alanna shivered, letting the Bazhir help her to her feet. "I doubt that I would be fit for such a life," she said dryly. "To carry all those memories every day? No, indeed!"

Halef Seif chuckled as he led her out of the

tent. "Not many are called to the life of the Voice, if that soothes you," he commented. "He will be here within the week." For a moment the tall Bazhir sighed, looking older than his years. "Between thee and me, woman of my tribe," he said quietly, "I hope the Voice will aid me to a fair solution in this matter of Ibn Nazzir. The old man disturbs the tribe's balance between headman and shaman; it cannot end well." He grimaced. "Come. There are tales you have not heard. Before I forget his message, the Voice asks me to say that you have met him, in the Sunset Room of Persopolis Castle."

The Sunset Room? she thought, startled. *The governor of Persopolis Castle! What was his name? Ali Mukhtab. He took us there, me and Jon and Raoul, Alex, Gary. He was the one who told us about the Black City. He was tall, with a nice vest, and intense eyes. Jon asked him for a written history of the Bazhir—*

"Ali Mukhtab?" she whispered in shock. "*Ali Mukhtab* is this 'Voice of the Tribes'?"

"He is," Halef Seif confirmed. "What better man to keep watch over the castle, where our oldest records are kept? Come. For now, become a member of the tribe. The Voice will be here in seven days. He will answer your questions then."

∾

Halef Seif was a man of his word. Alanna and Coram were returning from a hunt with the young

men of the tribe a week later when Faithful trotted
out from the village to meet them.

He's here, he yowled to Alanna in their private
language. *The Voice of the Tribes. He has very good
taste: he likes cats.*

"I know he likes cats, and I don't think that's an
indication of good taste," Alanna replied, leading
Moonlight to her hitching place with the tribe's
other horses. "Who's with him now?"

The shaman, Faithful replied. *One of his women
friends lured Halef Seif away with a lie about a quarrel in her household.*

"The news isn't good?" Coram asked quietly as
they rubbed their horses down.

Alanna shook her head. "Ibn Nazzir's stolen a
march on us with Ali Mukhtab."

Coram raised his thick brows. "The Voice of the
Tribes? But weren't ye sayin' ye were friends once?"

Alanna shrugged, leading the way to her tent.
"That was six years ago. He may have changed. I
don't know if he was this 'Voice of the Tribes' then."
She opened her tent flap and stopped, astounded at
the five bundles piled neatly inside. "What in the
Name of—"

"It is the first written history of the Bazhir."
The smooth voice behind them made Alanna and
Coram jump; they turned to face Ali Mukhtab. The
Voice of the Tribes wore a flowing blue burnoose
tied with a darker blue cord: religious colors among
the Bazhir, Alanna remembered. He was the same

as when she had seen him last: tall, with walnut-colored skin and a neatly trimmed mustache, his large hooded eyes framed with long curly lashes. He bowed now, his well-carved mouth turning up in a very small smile.

Remembering her manners, Alanna invited him in. She was just wondering how she would offer hospitality to her distinguished guest when Kara and Ishak arrived, bearing chilled wine and fruit. They presented their offerings first to Mukhtab, then to Alanna and Coram, before taking up stations just outside the tent flap. Mukhtab chuckled.

"I see you have been adopted," he commented. "Those are two of the three young ones you've bewitched?"

"She hasn't bewitched anyone," Coram growled, emptying his cup with one gulp. "Ibn Nazzir's a dried-up, jealous old man."

"This is Coram Smythesson," Alanna explained to the Bazhir. "He taught me the basics of the knight's art, and he looked after me when I was a page."

For a moment Coram received the full power of Mukhtab's eyes as the Bazhir opened them wide, examining him from top to toe. Oddly, the burly man turned red. "She's Trebond," he said as if answering a question. "Smythessons have served Trebond for generations."

"You have always been blessed in your friends,"

Ali Mukhtab said to Alanna. "I suppose by now you are aware of it." Alanna nodded, blushing herself. "And so you are a knight, and you have told all that you are female. But you are not happy?"

Alanna fiddled nervously with the ember-stone around her neck. "I have a few things on my mind."

She didn't object when the man reached over and picked the ember from her fingers, examining it. At last he sighed and let her tuck it back beneath her shirt. "The favored of the gods always have much on their minds," he admitted. "The shaman says I am an unnatural leader because I will not order you slain. He thinks you have bewitched me. Is this so?" He was smiling. Suddenly Alanna felt as if a burden had been taken from her. This enigmatic man was still her friend, for whatever reasons.

Coram snorted with derision. "And when did she have time to do that?"

Mukhtab nodded. "I asked the same question, but received no satisfactory answer. When I inquired how the Voice of the Tribes may order the slaying of a member of the tribe without full cause under law and a just hearing before the fire, Ibn Nazzir told me the Nameless Gods would have my soul for their enjoyment." The Bazhir shrugged. "The law is the law; he knows this as well as any." His eyes were serious as he looked at Alanna. "He wants you dead, Alanna of Trebond."

"He had his chance when Hakim fought me,"

she replied carelessly. "I don't understand why he's making a fuss now."

"You are a terrifying creature," the Voice told her solemnly. "You do not take your place in your father's tent, letting men make your decisions. You ride as a man, you fight as a man, and you think as a man—"

"I think as a human being," she retorted hotly. "Men don't think any differently from women— they just make more noise about being able to."

As Coram chuckled, Mukhtab said, "Have you not discovered that when people, men and women, find a woman who acts intelligently, they say she acts like a man?"

Alanna could find no answer to this. She glared at the guffawing Coram.

"Many of those who take the shaman's leadership are women," Mukhtab went on. "You frighten them. You are too new; you are too different. Will they have to behave differently, now that you are of the tribe? Better that you die and become a legend. Legends force no one to change."

"This is too silly for words," Alanna snapped. "Why have you brought this history to me?" She waved at the bundled scrolls.

"Six years ago Prince Jonathan indicated he would be interested in a written history of the Bazhir," Mukhtab explained. "Since your return to the North, my people and I have labored long on just such a written record. Our tribes are very old.

These scrolls tell all our story, from the time before we left our farms across the Inland Sea. We ask you to see that the Prince get them, as soon as possible. It is—vital." He looked at Coram. "May I speak with her alone?"

Coram struggled to his feet and left.

Alanna watched him go before asking, "Why is it vital? I hadn't planned to return to the palace for a long time." *If ever,* she thought with a terrible feeling of homesickness.

"It is vital," Ali Mukhtab whispered, leaning close, "because the end of my life draws near. Before I complete my last illness, Prince Jonathan must become the Voice of the Tribes."

three

Bazhir Shaman

*F*or a moment Alanna stared at the Voice. Finally she tried a weak grin. "You're joking, of course."

"I have never been more serious."

Alanna shook her head. "I think you had better explain it to me."

"Certain tribes have been at war with the King in the North for two generations," Mukhtab began. "The cost has been great for both sides. Among our people there is bitterness between those who accept your King and those who do not. And in the end, the Northern King must win."

"How do you know?" Alanna wanted to know.

"A small Gift of prophecy is given to each Voice," was the reply. "Your King will win if we continue to fight, because this time the Balance is weighed in his favor. Conquered, my people—*our* people, now—would be driven from the desert that is mother and father to us. All those things that enable us to make war against the King and against the hillmen who are our enemies would be taken away. The tribes would be scattered; we would be one people no more.

"But if Prince Jonathan were to become the Voice of the Tribes, he would be King one day—a *Bazhir* King. He would know us as we do ourselves. The tribes you call 'renegade' would make peace, for none may war against the Voice of the Tribes. They will make peace, and the Voice will bring them into Tortall without bloodshed.

"We must accept the King in the North; there is no other way. But we can do it so that we never forget who we are. Prince Jonathan is the key. With my passing, he will be the Voice, and my people will be safe."

Alanna nibbled at her thumb, considering. "Maybe Jon won't want to do it," she said at last. "The position seems to carry a lot of heartache to me."

Ali Mukhtab smiled. "Jonathan was born to rule, as you were born to make your own way. If there is any way he can better govern his people, he will take it. I have watched him for years. He will not turn his back on such power." Reaching into his robe, he brought out a thick letter sealed with wax. "Will you send this and the history to him, and let him make the choice?"

Alanna took the letter. Mukhtab was right: Jon had to make this decision himself. "I'll see that he gets it."

∽

Coram shook his head even as he pulled on his riding boots. "I don't like leavin' ye right now," he protested for the twentieth time. "That Akhnan Ibn Nazzir would feed ye to the wolves as soon as look at ye, and ye're sendin' me back to Corus."

"The sooner you ride to Corus, the sooner you'll be back to look out for me," Alanna said implacably. "This is important."

"Keepin' ye safe from that old buzzard isn't?" Coram demanded. "Ye said Mukhtab's sendin' a man with me?"

"He's waiting with the packhorse now," Alanna said, giving her friend an affectionate grin as they walked outside. "I'll be all right. I have Faithful to look after me."

Coram scowled at the black cat, who was trotting ahead. "Some protection," he muttered. They halted, surprised to see Hakim Fahrar waiting with the horses. The tall Bazhir bowed.

"I am to ride with you," he said in response to the question on their faces. "The Voice has said it."

Alanna hugged Coram for a moment. "You'll be back before you know it," she said gruffly. "So leave!"

She watched the two men ride off, their packhorse trailing behind. Fingering the ember at her throat, she blinked her watering eyes.

You're not alone, Faithful remarked. *You have me still.*

Alanna picked the cat up and hugged him tightly. She wasn't crying simply because she felt lost without Coram: the gruff manservant would be with Jonathan soon, and she wouldn't.

～

*T*he Ordeal. *She dropped through endless stretches of water, her lungs bursting for lack of air. She fought and fought, but she couldn't find her way to the surface. She opened her mouth to scream—*

She jerked awake, her mouth clamped shut so tightly that her jaws ached. She was forbidden to scream in the Chamber of the Ordeal!

Faithful fell to the ground from her chest. It had been his weight that made her sleeping mind remember that awful moment. About to yell her fury, she realized Faithful's tail and fur were erect. Keeping silent for a moment, she heard a rustle of movement, the soft click of hard objects striking each other gently.

Carefully Alanna lifted her battle-axe from her weapons rack and—moving soundlessly—she slid out the back of the tent. With Faithful behind, she circled her home, a shadow among the camp's other shadows.

A huddled figure was drawing designs before her door. She suddenly knew who it was, and could guess what he was up to. Hefting the axe, she hurled it into the sand at Akhnan Ibn Nazzir's feet, then strode forward, the violet fire of her Gift turning the scene into purple daylight.

"Demon, I adjure thee, harm me not!" the old man screeched. "In the name of Mithros—"

"Be quiet!" Alanna snapped as people ran out

of their tents, armed with swords and spears. "Now you've awakened everyone!"

Recognizing her at last, Ibn Nazzir gasped in fury. "I will cast you out!" he yelled. "I will cleanse our tribe of you and send you back into the Darkness where you belong!"

Examining the design the shaman had been working on, Alanna felt sick. It was called a Gate of Idramm: she had learned of it from Duke Roger, who had taught her and Jonathan sorcery when they were young.

"There are many kinds of creatures in our world," the Duke of Conté had explained. "Call them demons, elementals, spirits—their variety is infinite. Some serve that force we call Good, some that called Evil. A Gate of Idramm summons all such entities within a certain range. The result—" He had shrugged his broad shoulders. "Is disastrous. Only fools construct a Gate without putting limits on it."

This one was almost complete. Alanna shuddered. There were no limiting spells in the symbols of the design. "You stupid, ignorant, vicious old man!" she cried, scuffing it out with her bare foot. "You could have destroyed the entire village! Or didn't you care as long as you took me with you?"

Ali Mukhtab had come to the fore of the watching people; she snapped at him, "He was doing a Gate of Idramm!"

The Voice turned white. "Are you mad?" he

demanded of Akhnan Ibn Nazzir. "How dare you use sorcery you do not understand?"

"She is corrupting our people," the shaman whined. "She has corrupted you, Ali Mukhtab. I wished only to rid the desert of her evil—"

"You would have rid the desert of us all!" hissed Mukhtab furiously. "Go to your tent, shaman! Remain there until I have chosen a fitting punishment for you!" As the old man fled, he turned to Alanna. "You have saved us all," he told her.

Alanna pointed to Faithful, who blinked sleepily. "Thank my cat," she said. "He woke me up."

∾

When she left her bed the next morning, Ishak, Kara, and Kourrem awaited her, vying for Faithful's purrs. "You'll spoil him," Alanna said gruffly as she dressed. "And I'm the one who'll have to live with a spoiled cat."

"The men of the tribe do not believe he is a cat," Ishak told her. "Some think he is a god. Some think he is a demon."

"He's neither," Alanna informed him. She picked up Lightning. "Why doesn't one of you show me where the blacksmith is?"

The blacksmith was Gammal, her large friend from Persopolis. He grinned at the chance to do her a service, scowled at the girls until they backed out of the way, and handed a bellows to Ishak. "Use it well, boy," he advised as he turned to find his tongs.

Ishak looked at Alanna, terrified. "I've never done this," he whispered.

When Gammal returned, Alanna was busily pumping the bellows, bringing the fire to a white heat. The large Bazhir shook his head and picked up the long portion of Lightning's blade with his tongs, thrusting the metal into the fire until he judged it hot enough. Alanna thought she heard an ugly hum, but Gammal distracted her, booming, "Where did you learn to use the bellows, Woman Who Rides Like a Man?"

"From the King's weapons-masters," she shouted over the roar of the fire and the wheezing bellows. "We were at war with Tusaine. I was crippled with a wound, so I went to them to keep busy."

"Could you mend the sword yourself?" the smith wanted to know. Even he had to raise his voice to be heard over the noise from the forge.

Alanna shook her head. "I could mend an ordinary sword," she called, "but not one so well made."

Gammal pulled the length of metal from the forge and she put up the bellows. Without the wheezing, she could clearly hear the humming sound from Lightning's sheared-off blade. "Gammal, don't—" she began, but the smith was striking. His hammer met the glowing metal; everyone was knocked down by the resulting explosion. When Alanna struggled to her feet, the fire was out, the anvil was cracked down the center, and Gammal was unconscious. She brought him around quickly with water fetched by Kourrem, and the Bazhir grinned.

That was a mistake, Faithful commented from a safe distance away. *Look at the blade.*

Lightning still lay on the anvil. After a moment Alanna touched it; the broken piece was as cold as the forge. "It was not meant to be struck by a hammer," Ali Mukhtab's voice said unexpectedly. Alanna spun, startled because she had not heard the Voice come up behind her. "You must find some other way to repair it, Alanna of Trebond." He smiled suddenly, his white teeth flashing. "The people of this tribe lived very quietly before you came," he commented, before turning and walking away.

Alanna scowled at the Voice's retreating back, before she realized that Kara, Ishak, and Kourrem were giggling. "He is right," Kara said. "But we are glad you came."

With a sigh Alanna slid the broken length of sword back into its sheath, strapping the hilt into place once more. She would have to find some other way to repair it. Her lessons in sorcery had not included sword-smithing. And what was she to do for a sword until then? She felt unprepared without Lightning in her hand.

"Those three should be glad that you have come among us," Gammal commented softly. Alanna looked sharply around for her attendants: they were some distance away, trying to interest Faithful in a brightly colored ball. "Before they had little status. Come into my tent, and my woman will give you something cool to drink," he added. "The young ones can look after your cat, and each other, for now."

Alanna followed the smith into his living quarters, gnawing thoughtfully at her thumb. Gammal's wife served them, her eyes nervous over her veil. "Why?" Alanna finally asked. "They're intelligent, alert, quick—I like them. Why would they have little status?"

Gammal lit a pipe, drawing on it thoughtfully before answering. "The boy Ishak claimed he saw pictures in the fire when he was only six," he replied.

"Of course," Alanna said, puzzled. "He told me himself he has the Gift. He hasn't had much instruction for someone his age—"

Gammal waved this aside. "Balls of brightly colored fire hung over Kourrem's bed, and she played with them. Kara throws things without touching them when she is angry. The shaman says they are cursed. Ishak's family left their son to the teaching of his grandfather, but the families of the girls cast them out as soon as they could fend for themselves."

Alanna could not believe she had heard correctly. "But—all those things are signs of the Gift—of magic," she whispered. "And Ibn Nazzir said they were *cursed?*"

Gammal nodded. "Some in the tribe think the

shaman has made a mistake. They look after the three, clothing them and feeding them. Halef Seif is one such."

"I suppose you're another," Alanna guessed shrewdly.

Gammal ducked his head in acknowledgment as she turned her mind to another problem. "Does this mean the girls have never been trained? They don't know how to use their power?" Gammal shook his head. "Great Merciful Mother," Alanna breathed. "I'd rather live in a pit of snakes than in the same village with two girls who don't know how to control their sorcery! Doesn't anyone realize what could happen? They must have learned *some* control, or none of you would be here. But haven't you noticed anything peculiar, when one of them is angry or sick?"

Gammal nodded, unperturbed. "Once lightning came out of the sky and almost struck the shaman," he said. "And there are always great winds and strange storms. The shaman says we should kill them at such times, but Halef Seif will not permit it. The Voice will not permit it. And so they live here, until the Balance shifts in their favor."

Soon after this Alanna took her leave. The Bazhir were very willing simply to let things happen, which was strange in such an energetic people. Didn't they realize that the only way to change things was to act? She tried to express her confusion to Ali Mukhtab, to his amusement.

"We believe in the Great Balance," he told her. "All will right itself in the end. The Balance shifts—it cannot be predicted. It is like the desert, you see. The sands drift always, yet the desert remains the same. Man cannot change the desert, and man cannot affect the Balance."

Alanna shook her head with exasperation. "I don't believe in waiting for things to just *happen*," she growled. "If I waited for your Balance to right itself, I'd be some lord's wife right now, not knowing anything more than my home and my lands."

"And perhaps you are an instrument of the Balance," Mukhtab suggested. "By your very presence, you cause the scales to shift."

"Nonsense," Alanna replied, fingering the ember-stone at her throat.

⌒

*H*er three friends were on Alanna's mind for several days. They weren't bitter or depressed about their lot, and their endless questions spoke for a willingness to learn. She would have tried to teach them herself, just for her own peace of mind, but Bazhir custom was very strict about such things. Instruction in magic was done by the shaman: only in this tribe, where the shaman was uncertain of what little magic he *did* have, was no one instructed at all. Not even Ali Mukhtab would defend her if she broke all Bazhir customs.

The wistful look in Kourrem's eyes tugged at

Alanna's heart. Ishak never stopped trying to show her his magic. And Kara was Kara, anxious, ready to please, expecting a curt word or a blow rather than Alanna's gruff thanks. The knight had been something of an outcast since the day she had revealed her secret; she didn't like that life for her young shadows. Although her southern exile was voluntary, she had few illusions about the welcome that would be hers if she returned to the palace too soon.

She fretted over it for nearly a week as she learned about her new tribe: meeting its men with Halef Seif, discussing the constant war with the hillmen and the need for new forage for their many herds of sheep and goats; meeting a few women with Kara; hunting with the young men; discovering the rich history of the Bazhir with Ali Mukhtab.

Alanna was still considering what to do when she was summoned to the headman's tent one night. The Voice of the Tribes was there, enthroned on pillows and smoking his long pipe. Halef Seif, looking stern, was at his side. Gammal and another man stood over two bound and kneeling strangers while other men of the tribe looked on.

Alanna hesitated in the doorway, resettling Faithful on her left shoulder. "You sent for me?" she asked Halef. Everyone but the two kneeling men had turned to stare at her.

The headman beckoned her forward. "These two came yesterday to our brothers in the Tribe of the Sleeping Lion," he explained. "They tried to pass as desertmen, when it is plain they are northerners."

Alanna walked forward, trying to see the captives' faces. Both looked down. "Surely the men of the Sleeping Lion are able to look after spies," she suggested, still not knowing why she had been called. "Unless they felt the Voice should see them?"

"These men asked questions about *you*, Alanna of Trebond," replied Ali Mukhtab.

Faithful leaped from Alanna's shoulder. Walking over to one of the kneeling men, the cat lazily butted against his face. Startled, the man looked up.

"'Fingers!" Alanna cried, startled. "What in the Name of the Mother are *you* doing here?"

The second man—one she had known only slightly from her days in the Court of the Rogue—looked up as well. The thief Alanna had known for years as "Lightfingers" grimaced.

"He said we weren't t'let you know we was here," he grumbled. "We was t'find out what'd happened to you, and if you was safe."

"Doubtless you will explain in your own time, Alanna," Halef remarked gently.

Red with embarrassment, Alanna faced him. "The master of these men is one of my oldest and greatest friends."

"Who might their master be, that he sends spies to us rather than messengers who declare their intent openly?"

Alanna sighed. "He's the master of the Court of the Rogue, the King of the Thieves in Tortall. If you knew him, you'd know he always sends spies rather than messengers." She turned back to 'Fingers. "Why on earth is he looking for me? Surely he knows I'm all right."

'Fingers shook his head. "I'm not the one t'question his Majesty," he informed Alanna. "Not of late in particular, when he's turned that testy. We knew we'd be caught, but—" He shrugged. "'Twas better far than stayin' in Corus, when George is in a temper."

Alanna smiled. "I've never seen George in a temper, but he's formidable enough the rest of the time. Halef Seif, Ali Mukhtab, don't hold these two responsible for their master's orders. Disobeying George—the King of the Thieves—well, if you're a thief it's something you just don't do."

Removing his pipe from his mouth, Ali Mukhtab said, "I have heard of this George Cooper. As you say, he is a hard man to cross."

"Surely these two haven't seen anything the Bazhir wouldn't want them to see," Alanna pointed out.

"It is your will that they be released?" Halef Seif asked the Voice. Ali Mukhtab nodded, and Gammal knelt to cut the ropes binding the captives. "Listen to me," Halef told them sternly. "You return to your King of Thieves unmarked and unharmed, but for a little rough handling. His next spies I will return to him with slit nostrils." He nodded to Gammal. "Feed them and send them on their way. Make certain they are well on the road to the north before you return to us."

"Tell George I'm well and content," Alanna added as 'Fingers and his companion rose awkwardly. "I just need to live my own life for a while."

Lightfingers nodded. "I'll tell him, but I doubt he'll like it."

His companion looked around at the Bazhir. "He may have to," he remarked dryly. They were hurried from the tent, the warriors following.

Alanna discovered Halef Seif and Ali Mukhtab were looking at her. At a gesture from the headman, she sat. Halef drew up his own pipe stand and sat as well, while a young tribesman who had stayed behind poured wine for each of them.

"Are there other such friends who will come seeking you, Alanna?" Ali Mukhtab wanted to know.

She shook her head. "George is a law to himself."

"How did you come to know such a one?" The Voice gave Halef a light from his pipe.

"We met when I first arrived in Corus, disguised as a boy," she replied. "He became my friend—"

"So he could steal in the palace," Halef suggested dryly.

"Not at all. I never would've helped him to

steal. As it was, he taught me knife-fighting, how to climb walls without a ladder—" She grinned. "All manner of useful things. And he got Moonlight for me."

The Voice's eyes were sharp. "He must be close to you, this—"

"George Cooper," she supplied. "He's my best friend in the world, next to Prince Jonathan."

"This friend goes to great risk, sending messengers south to find you."

Alanna blushed. "George worries about me," she mumbled.

George loves you, Faithful yowled.

"Hush," she snapped, seeing the two men look at her cat. Sometimes people could understand Faithful; she didn't want this to be one of those times. She rose, nearly tripping over her burnoose. "If that's everything—"

"For now," the headman nodded, barely hiding a smile behind his hand.

～

The incident was soon forgotten, and shortly afterward Alanna decided to approach Ibn Nazzir on behalf of Kara, Kourrem, and Ishak. She had not crossed verbal swords with the shaman in days, and she hoped his rage had cooled. Leaving her weapons and her cool burnoose behind, wearing a sleeveless tunic and breeches (so the old man could see clearly she was unarmed), Alanna went to beard him in his tent at noon.

As always Faithful accompanied her, a coal-black, complaining shadow. *This is a fool's errand,* he warned her as they approached the shaman's home. *He will scream and call you names, and probably he'll try some spell he knows nothing about.*

"I have to try," Alanna muttered as she stepped onto the wide bare spot before the tent that served the tribe as temple and as the shaman's home. She stood a discreet distance from the covered opening, spread her hands wide so all could see they were empty. "Akhnan Ibn Nazzir! I have come to you in peace, with open—"

The ground before her exploded, knocking her and Faithful down and showering them both with dirt and sand.

I told you so, Faithful remarked disgustedly as he began to wash.

Alanna got to her feet, brushing herself off as she fought to hold on to her temper. "That was stupid!" she yelled. "Someone might have been hurt, and it wouldn't have been me! I came to you willing to make peace—"

"You will make nothing among us but war and famine!" came the muffled scream from the tent. "You corrupt Halef Seif with lust; your vile words have bewitched the Voice of the Tribes!"

"Men and women can be friends without lust!" Alanna yelled back. "The only person who's bewitched around here is you, bewitched by your

own jealousy and stupidity!" She stopped to wipe
sweat off her forehead, trembling with anger. Her
tolerance for fools had always been slight, and she
was losing the little she had.

Still the old man refused to come out, although
the exchange was drawing the rest of the village.
"You carry the eye of a demon around your throat!"

Alanna put her hand to her throat and touched
the ember-stone. "It is not the eye of a demon!" she
cried with fury. "It is a token given me by the Great
Mother Goddess, from Her own hand!" Those listening drew back, awed and frightened. The
Mother was as well known and worshipped here as
she was in the north; none of them would use Her
name lightly. Those who followed the shaman
began to wonder if they had made a very bad mistake.

"I want an apology for your insult to my
Goddess!" she yelled, her voice getting hoarse. "I
demand it right now! Come out and make it!"

There, she thought with satisfaction, balancing
on the balls of her feet. *That ought to settle the old
coward.*

Faithful was facing the shaman's tent, his ears
pricked forward. Suddenly his tail began to twitch.
He's not going to apologize, he warned as the tent
flap stirred. *He's going to—*

But Alanna could feel it as well as the cat. There
was just time for her to throw up defensive walls as
yellow flame roared from the tent, surrounding her

and Faithful. She flinched as it struck, holding her mind fixed on her own spell. Angry—with Ibn Nazzir's ignorance and lack of control, a bystander could have been hurt or killed—she seized the last bit of fire and threw it back. The tiny flame rushed into the shaman's tent and chased the old man outside before vanishing.

Alanna glared at Ibn Nazzir, thinking rapidly. He was wearing the crystal sword; the sight of it sent cold fear down her back. Not only was she concerned about anything that reminded her of Roger of Conté, she knew the shaman had been a rider once. Doubtless he could use a sword. Unless she was mistaken, she was more than his match as a sorceress, but his fencing skills were a dangerous unknown, particularly since she was unarmed.

"You insult the Goddess who shows me favor," she said when she had his attention. "You attacked me twice without provocation and without fair warning. I've been more than patient with you. Tell me why I shouldn't demand your life, as is my right as a member of this tribe."

Akhnan Ibn Nazzir drew the crystal sword and rushed Alanna with a yell.

She dodged and circled away, deaf to the furious shouts from the tribesmen at the shaman's disregard for honor. Ibn Nazzir, at the end of his sanity, was also deaf to them. His mouth set in a crazy grin, he rushed Alanna again, wielding that deadly blade with both hands.

The woman knight ducked away, moving easily on the packed dirt. She could *feel* the crystal sword humming each time it sliced past her. The sound made her slightly ill: it was as if Duke Roger were nearby, directing the sword in its quest for her life. Empty-handed, intent on the shaman's moves, she wove and danced away as he slashed at her.

Ibn Nazzir was not the opponent Duke Roger had been. His swings were often wild; he was badly balanced and slow. It was the sword Alanna feared; she had a feeling the old man would not have been as good as he was now without it. Gripping the ember-stone, she whispered a wall-building spell.

Violet fire sprang into being, whirling to encircle Ibn Nazzir. He shrieked and swept the sword around him; the wall vanished. He charged; Alanna jumped, kicking him to the ground. With a roll she was on him, wrestling for the sword. The humming was louder, drowning out all other sound. Invisible fingers gripped her throat even as she saw the shaman start to turn gray.

"Stop it!" she yelled, trying to make herself heard. With a corner of her mind she gripped the magical fingers, holding them away from her. "You don't have the strength: you're using your own life-force!"

He knocked her onto her back. Alanna clung to the sword's hilt; at this range he couldn't miss once he got the blade free. They struggled, drops of sweat falling onto her face from him. He was turning grayer, and there were blue lines around his mouth and nostrils.

Everything went black. The cloud that suddenly enfolded Alanna cut off all air and feeling. She fought, drawing on reserves of strength that had been built up over years of work and subterfuge. Slowly her own violet fire shoved the blackness away, sparking and flaring where it touched the crystal blade. In the distance she heard a cry.

The blackness was gone. Akhnan Ibn Nazzir collapsed against her, his eyes wide and staring in death.

Gammal and Halef pulled the old man off her, and Ishak helped her to her feet. Alanna swayed with exhaustion; Kara and Kourrem hurried forward to support her on either side. Ali Mukhtab looked up from his examination of Ibn Nazzir's body, his dark eyes puzzled. "There is no mark on him, yet he is dead. What caused it?"

Alanna rubbed her eyes. She had expended much of her strength, physical and magical. Just now she only wanted to go to her tent and lie down. "He was using power he didn't have," she rasped finally. "He wasn't that good a sorcerer. He tapped his own life-force because he wanted me dead." Looking at her right hand, she was stunned to realize she held the crystal sword. "If he could've lasted, maybe he would've won. But I lasted. I usually do," she added bitterly. "I'm sorry I brought trouble to you." She started to turn away.

"One moment." Halef's voice was kind but firm. She looked back to see him pointing at the shaman's tent. "This is your home now."

Alanna braced her free hand on Kourrem's shoulder. "I don't understand."

Ali Mukhtab rose to stand beside the headman. "Halef Seif is right. You have slain the old shaman. You must now take his place until you teach a new shaman, or until one slays you."

It was too much. "That's crazy!" Alanna shouted, her voice cracking with weariness. "I'm not—I'm a knight! I've never taught sorcery—"

"Would you leave us defenseless against the shamans of the hillmen?" Halef asked quietly. Alanna closed her mouth, remembering the Bazhir tales of the hill-sorcerers. "That is the law. That is our custom." He opened the door flap of the shaman's tent. "This is your home now, Woman Who Rides Like a Man."

For a moment Alanna's violet eyes met those of the Voice and of the headman fiercely. She did not want to spend time bound to one place; she was searching for adventure! Another wave of exhaustion swept her, and she looked away. Faithful sat expectantly before the open door, waiting.

"I don't care if it's home or a grave-digger's hut," she sighed. "I just want a place to lie down." With Kara and Kourrem supporting her, still clutching the crystal sword, she entered the shaman's tent.

four

Studies in Sorcery

One of Alanna's first acts as shaman of the Bloody Hawk was to approach Ali Mukhtab and Halef Seif about training replacements: Kara, Kourrem, and Ishak. "Ishak knows some magic," she told them. "And all three must've developed some control, or this village wouldn't be here still. It doesn't take much learning to be a shaman, and they would be better than Ibn Nazzir ever was."

The men thought her proposal over for long moments, their faces unreadable. Alanna tried to keep from fidgeting. Where would she find other likely candidates, if she couldn't train these three? Also, giving the outcasts shaman status would go a long way toward redressing the wrong Ibn Nazzir had done them, to her way of thinking.

"To make girls shamans is a new thing," Ali Mukhtab said at last. "But this tribe has done many things that are new since the coming of the Woman Who Rides Like a Man."

"Our shaman now is also a woman," Halef added, smiling just a little.

"You like this, then?" Mukhtab asked. The

headman's smile broadened. "I think it will be very interesting to watch. Certainly the young ones will obey *this* shaman."

Mukhtab nodded. "It will be done," he told Alanna. "May the gods smile on you."

Alanna levered herself to her feet. "Thank you," she said. "I'm probably going to need the gods smiling on me."

The three were waiting for her when she returned to the tent. Alanna looked around, satisfied. The place looked very different from the way it had the afternoon she had first lurched inside. Brass and silver shone softly in the lamplight. The carpets glowed in their original deep colors. The hangings that separated the temple from her living area were spotless. *It's actually pleasant to come home to,* she thought.

"You asked us to wait for you here," Kourrem, ever forthright, told her. "You talked with the headman and the Voice. Are we in trouble?"

Alanna shook her head, accepting the date wine Ishak poured for her. "We were talking about you, yes," she replied. "But you aren't in trouble. I wanted their permission to train you as shamans. They said I could."

For a moment three pairs of eyes—the girls' dark-brown, the boy's brownish-gray—stared at her. Kourrem started to cry.

"I thought you didn't wish to talk about magic, ever," Ishak reminded her, puzzled.

Kara had joined Kourrem, upsetting Alanna.

"Girls, stop that. I didn't mean to make you cry; drink some of this wine." She told Ishak, "I said that without knowing the girls hadn't been trained at all, and you only a little. Kourrem, Kara, *please* don't cry. Yes, I'm sick of magic; but someone has to teach you three, and I'm it. Listen to me." She sat down on a pillow with a sigh. The girls were reduced to sniffles; she had everyone's attention. "While I was a page, then a squire, in the palace, there was a man—the King's nephew, my Prince's cousin. Duke Roger was the greatest sorcerer in the Eastern Lands. He was handsome, well-liked, charming. I felt I was the only person in the world who knew he meant my Prince no good, that he caused accidents that nearly killed Jonathan. I think he had me kidnapped by the enemy when we fought Tusaine. Then, when I took the Ordeal of Knighthood two moons ago, I learned he had used his sorcery to blind everyone—including me, in a way—to his plans. He wanted to kill the Queen. I accused him before the King and the entire Court. Roger demanded a trial by combat."

She drew a deep breath. This was painful. "We fought. He—cut through—" She blushed, unsure of what to say. "I had disguised myself as a boy—" She waved her hands around her chest area, turning redder than before.

Quick-witted Kourrem saved her. "You mean you bound your chest so it was flat, and he cut through the binding."

Alanna nodded. "When he found out—when

everyone found out—that I was a girl, he went crazy. He attacked with a sword *and* with magic, but he didn't attack just me. His sorcery would've killed the King, or Jonathan. I had to stop him, so I killed him. Ever since then, I've felt magic—any kind of magic—is too easily used for evil." She drew a deep breath. "But ignoring magic is worse. It's like this crystal sword." She touched the blade she now wore at her waist. "I ignored it, and Ibn Nazzir was able to turn it against me. I have to keep it for myself, and master it, so it can never be used against me again. That's what you three must learn to do with *your* magic, or it will turn on you." She rubbed her nose, embarrassed. She was not one for speeches. She was just realizing that she had let herself in for a large number of them. "We start in the morning. You'd best get your sleep."

The next minute she was drowning in gleeful teenagers who insisted on hugging and kissing her. She shooed them out and closed the tent flap for the night, shaking her head. "This training will be good for them," she told Faithful as she prepared to go to bed.

The cat watched her, his tail twitching lazily. *It will be good for you, too,* he commented. *It might even make an adult of you, but I doubt that.*

Alanna glared at him as she wound herself into her blankets. "I'm glad I have you to keep me humble," she muttered as she readied herself for sleep.

I'm glad you do, too, Faithful replied, settling himself by her nose.

∾

The tomb was dark and still. Behind her the door was sealed shut by a slab of rock the palace servants had placed there. Before her, on a granite block, lay the body of Duke Roger of Conté. He looked as if he slept, well preserved by the arts of the Black God's priests. His black velvet tunic hid the shoulder wound and the thrust through his chest that had ended her duel with him. There was no sound in the tomb. He was dead.

His eyes snapped open. She stepped back, her heart thudding with horror. He smiled.

Alanna threw her covers aside and rolled out of bed, shaking. Lurching to her feet, she ran out of the tent with Faithful just behind her. Once outside she stood panting in the cold night breeze, feeling chills as it struck her sweat-soaked body.

∾

"The first magic you learn is fire-making," she told her pupils. They were in the desert not far from the village. Alanna didn't want to be near people or tents, in case of accidents. A warrior of the tribe stood a safe distance away, his bow strung and ready. The hillmen were too near for anyone to risk going far without a guard.

Alanna put a twig down on top of several others. "It's easy for anyone who has the Gift at all to make a fire or to create light," she went on, feeling uncomfortable. She had taught combat arts to pages and squires before, but never sorcery; she was worried that she might do something wrong. "You look at what you want to burn—later you won't have to look at it—and you picture it burning. Then you *want* it to burn."

"What if I don't want it to burn?" Kara asked.

"You *have* to want it to burn," Alanna said. "Otherwise why would you be trying this spell?"

"Oh."

"The source of all your magic lies in your own will," Alanna continued. "Things happen because you want them to. It's like anything else in life —becoming a warrior, or a good shaman, or a good cook—it will happen if you want it badly enough. If you focus your will, and see that thing burning in your mind, then what you want becomes real. The thing will burn. Kara, you try first."

The taller of the girls squinted at the pile of twigs, sweat pouring down her face as she concentrated. A tiny puff of smoke drifted up, but it soon died. "That's good for the first time," Alanna told her. "*I* couldn't raise a little smoke when I first tried. All right, Kourrem."

Kourrem scowled at the twigs; her eyebrows knitted together. At last she shook her head. "I don't think I want it badly enough." She sighed.

"You want to be a shaman, don't you?" Alanna asked her.

Kourrem's face lit up. "Yes!"

"You can't be a shaman if you can't do this. Even Akhnan Ibn Nazzir could light a fire."

Kourrem's eyes widened with alarm. In the next moment sparks flew from the pile of twigs.

Alanna grinned. "See?" She waited for the flurry of sparks to die out, then pointed to Ishak. "You next."

Grinning smugly, the youth pointed at the wood. It flared up in a spout of flame, instantly consumed. Alanna looked at him for a long moment, itching to slap the cocky look off his face. She knew the emotion was unworthy of her; Ishak had simply wanted to show off a little. Getting her temper under control, she nodded. "I forgot you already knew some fire-magic. Before we go any further, I'd better find out exactly what each of you can do."

"I can do fire and light," Ishak announced. "I can find things. Sometimes I can see things that are going to be."

"He dreamed that you would make our lives good," Kara put in eagerly. "We laughed at him because he said a woman who was a warrior would be the one. That was the day before Halef Seif brought you to our tribe."

Alanna nodded. "What about you, Kara? Have you seen things become different because you wanted them to? Do you see pictures in the fire?"

"Things move when I am angry," Kara whispered, blushing. "Sometimes they fly through the air. Then I am beaten."

"She makes the wind blow," Ishak volunteered. "And it rains when she cries. Not always, but sometimes."

"Weather magic," Alanna said. "As a shaman you'll find it useful. Kourrem?"

"I don't know," the youngest of them admitted. "Sometimes I see balls of colored fire, and I play with them. The old people like me to come when they're sick; they say I make them feel better. I thought it was because I tell them stories, but—" Her eyes were hopeful as she looked at Alanna.

Remembering how Duke Baird had tested her on the day Jonathan took the Sweating Sickness, Alanna held out her hand. "I slept badly last night," she told Kourrem. "I still feel tired. Take my hand and make me feel better."

Kourrem reached out, then pulled her hand back. "I don't know how."

"Find your own strength, and then shove some of it through your hand into me," Alanna instructed. "Go on."

Kourrem obeyed. The next moment Alanna felt a tingling energy flooding into her body, making the hair on the back of her neck stand straight up. She yanked her hand away, and shook the tingling out of it. "I was only a *little* tired," she told the girl, who looked as if she was about to cry. "You didn't need to give me so much!" She looked at them, bracing her hands on her hips. "We need to think about what you should learn," she admitted. "You each already know something, or you couldn't control your magic as well as you do."

"How do you know that?" Kara asked.

"Because Ishak could have burned up all four of us without any control," Alanna replied. "Because if you couldn't rein in your magic, the village would have been destroyed by winds or rain. And Kourrem could have blown me apart with what she did just now."

"Then why do you take such chances teaching us?" Kourrem demanded. "You didn't *know* I wouldn't hurt you, did you?"

Alanna grinned. "I may not be able to raise the weather or see the future, but I know something about protecting myself; and each of you, if I must." She scratched her head. "I think we'd better practice the focusing exercise I taught you. Then you're going to get the tents I asked for and set them up by mine."

"Why do you want us to set up tents?" Kara asked as they sat on the ground obediently.

Alanna settled beside them, crossing her legs beneath her. "As my apprentices, you should properly live with me," she replied. "But since there are three of you, I had the tentmaker give me one larger tent for the girls and one smaller one for

Ishak. Oh, stop that!" she cried as they threw themselves on her, hugging her frantically.

~

*A*fter the evening meal, the apprentices went to furbish up their new homes, and Halef Seif came for Alanna. "The night is cool," he told her. "Will you go riding with me?"

She didn't need to be asked twice. It took them a few moments to saddle their horses and tell the sentries which direction they planned to take. Once free of the village, Alanna drew a deep breath of relief. She could smell desert plants, dust, and horses—a dry, reassuring scent that told her more than anything else her life was very different these days.

"I want them to sit with me at the campfire," she said abruptly, keeping her voice low in case predators, animal or human, were near. "That's their right as my apprentices, isn't it?"

"Two of them are girls." There was little light with which to read his face, and his voice was bland.

"I'm a girl, too."

"I have noticed."

Alanna suspected him of teasing her. "I don't care if they're three-headed toads," she whispered tartly. "They're all going to be shamans, and the tribe must learn to—"

The Bazhir hissed for silence. Faithful was erect

in his cup on Moonlight's saddle, his fur standing up, his tail lashing. Alanna tuned her ears to the night sounds and heard it—rock falling against rock as men made their way through the small gorge just below. Soundlessly she and Halef Seif dismounted; with a touch, she made Faithful stay put. She followed the man to the edge of the gorge, where they flattened themselves on the ground, peering over.

Her eyes had adjusted to the moonless night, and now she could see the shadowy forms of five hillmen stealing along the ground below her. One tripped on a rock and cursed softly while his companions hushed him; Alanna sneered, knowing she would have received months of punishment duty if she had made such a mistake even as a page.

"Raiders looking for our herds." Halef's breath stirred the hair by her ear; had she been a few inches farther away she could not have heard him. "I think we will not disturb the guards." He made as if to rise, then flattened himself beside her once more. "Some light would be useful—shaman." He was smiling.

Swiftly Alanna reached inside herself, finding that small bit of fire that always burned deep where only she could find it. She drew the fire out, feeling a rush of excitement as it grew swiftly to meet her need. Violet-colored light burst from her palm, making everything brighter. The hillmen yelped, shielding their eyes. Halef Seif scrambled down into the gorge, screaming war cries. Pressed for time and needing both hands, Alanna looked around frantically. Spotting a stone, she pointed at it and gave her magic the command. She didn't know if it could be done, but there was no time to think. The violet fire streamed into the big rock, filling it as it had filled her. For a moment it seemed to flicker and die—then it became part of the stone, a huge beacon shining on the battleground below.

"Tortall and the King!" Alanna cried, following Halef Seif. She drew the crystal sword, feeling its ominous humming in her hand. Once more its magic reached out, seeking ways to take over her purpose, but Alanna was concentrating only on the hillmen attacking Halef Seif. She set her jaw and held on, mentally telling the sword, *Stop that.*

Two of them saw her and attacked, one with an axe, the other with a broadsword. She ducked under the swing of the axe-man and came up inside, running him through. For an instant sick, black triumph roared up into her mind. She froze, knowing the sword's magic was turning her fierce pride in being the better fighter into an ugly joy at killing. She trembled, fighting the desire to run the man through again and again, until Halef Seif yelled her name. She whirled in time to catch a descending broadsword on the crystal sword's hilt. The other sword was bigger and heavier, its owner larger and stronger than Alanna, but the strange gray blade held. It flickered with a ghostly light that caught the hillman's eyes. Alanna broke away and came back, cutting up and under. The hillman was still staring at her sword; he tried to block, but he was sluggish. The crystal sword flicked up and inside his guard, cutting deeply into his neck. This time she was ready for the rush of power from the sword; this time she struck back at it with her mind, tearing at its source. Had she been forced to describe it, she would have said that it felt like a knot in the threads of power that made up the sword's magic. Now her mind cut through the knot, pulling it out of the sword's makeup, hurling it into the night. The last of the would-be raiders had decided to run from the victorious Halef Seif; the evil Alanna had thrown away struck his back, turning him instantly into a pile of ashes.

"I didn't mean for that to happen," she whispered tiredly, wiping the blade on a fallen man's cloak. The sword's humming was less now, and the ugly triumph she had felt at killing was only a shadow on her memory.

"It is foolish to let such a one escape, to take reports to his tribe," the headman told her sternly. "And what *did* happen? You were not fighting with all of you." His sharp eyes took in the crystal sword as she resheathed it. "The sword is evil. It will turn on you."

She shook her head. "Very little that is real is evil, Halef Seif," she replied. "Magic itself isn't evil, but it can be turned to evil purposes. If you can straighten the magic out somehow—"

"And what if this sword's magic has been turned to evil for ages beyond count?" she was asked. "What if you are not strong enough to defeat it?"

Alanna poked her chin forward; her violet eyes glittered dangerously. "I've promised myself I will master this blade, and I *will*," she said between gritted teeth. "No sword—not even this one—is going to beat *me*." She whistled and Moonlight trotted down to her, Halef Seif's stallion following. She mounted up, still scowling at the headman. "And that is that!"

Hiding a smile, the Bazhir mounted his own steed. "As you say—Woman Who Rides Like a Man."

∿

*A*lanna had thought that her girl apprentices might protest their inclusion at the tribe's fire, but she had underestimated their awe of her. Once they realized Alanna would let them continue to wear face veils, they agreed. Kara looked frightened, and Kourrem set her jaw stubbornly, but both ranged themselves between Ishak and Alanna the next night, looking at the ground as silence fell. For a few moments nothing was said. Then the talk began again, slowly, as man after man shrugged his acceptance. It was the women who held back that night, and the next, and the next, serving the girls and Alanna with an abruptness that would have been rude if Halef Seif had not been watching. Alanna sighed. How could she get the tribe's women to accept her and her apprentices? She couldn't *force* them to like the changes she had brought to the Bloody Hawk.

Lessons continued, with all of them studying the scrolls on ceremonial magic that lay before the tribe's altars. Of the apprentices, Ishak did the best with these spells, which covered everything from cleansing the lamps to consecrating a new temple. Alanna watched her boy pupil's growing cockiness with apprehension. To her, used to the slightest quirks exhibited by the pages and squires she had once taught, it was plain that Ishak was getting dangerously over-confident.

"Can't you let me move ahead?" he demanded of Alanna one evening as the young shaman and her students relaxed in the common area of her tent. Kourrem was fussing over a loom she had set up, and Kara was helping to thread it; but Alanna could feel both girls listening hard. "I've already learned most of the ceremonial magic; can't you teach me something *interesting?*"

Alanna stroked Faithful. The cat sprawled over her lap, listening as intently as the girls. "Precisely what did you have in mind?"

"I'd like to learn spells for divination," he replied, his eyes shining. "I'd be able to see the future. Or you could teach me how to leave my body—"

"No, Ishak." She said it gently, knowing she was

disappointing him. "You aren't ready for what you're asking. I'm sorry."

"I think I *am* ready!" he retorted, his temper surfacing. He bit his lip, then went on more quietly. "Will you at least let me handle your sword? I could use its magic—"

Alanna shook her head. "No one handles it but me."

"I want something *exciting* to do!" he cried. "You won't let me handle your sword; you won't teach me advanced magic—"

"The spells you're talking about are strong and delicate. You don't have the discipline to proceed slowly. Ishak, listen to me!" she went on as he turned away. "Don't you know what happens when you attempt magic you aren't ready for? If you're lucky, the spell won't work. If you're unlucky, it will get out of hand and burn you up. If you tried to use the sword, it would consume you. You'd die, and nothing could bring you back. Learn to be patient. Stop trying to skip steps as you've been doing with the ritual spells—yes, I've seen you! With magic you *must* be careful."

"You're as bad as Akhnan Ibn Nazzir!" he burst out. "You have a cat that's supernatural, a token from the Goddess, a magic sword, the Gift—and you want to keep it all for yourself! You don't want anyone else to have fun!" He turned and ran out.

Alanna shook her head, troubled. "It's *not* 'fun,'" she murmured, more to herself than to

Faithful or the girls. She looked at her other anxiously watching apprentices and forced a smile. Ishak would cool off and find something new to be excited about in the morning—she hoped. "Does that thing work?" she asked Kourrem.

Eager to change the subject, the girl nodded. "I'm glad you let me set it up. I don't feel right, just sitting here in the evening when I could be weaving."

"Are you any good at it?" Alanna wanted to know.

Kourrem shook her head. "No, but I want to learn." She squinted at the threads. "I know a little."

"She knows more than a little," Kara announced. "She's a good weaver. It's important for a woman to do something well, so she can bring honor and good fortune into the tent of her husband," she added wisely.

"Are you two looking for husbands?" Alanna wanted to know.

"I'm not sure," Kara admitted, sitting and wrapping her arms around her knees. "While we were outcasts in the tribe, there was still a chance that a man from another tribe might want one of us as a wife. But now that we are shamans, it's hard to say. The shaman before Akhnan Ibn Nazzir had a wife, but Ibn Nazzir didn't—he was too dirty. Would a man want to marry a woman who is a shaman?"

Alanna remembered that Jonathan had asked

her to marry him. "As much as a man will want to marry a woman who is a warrior," she said reassuringly. "And I personally know two who wanted to marry me."

Kara's face lit up. "Kourrem, did you hear that?" she cried happily. "*Two* men wanted to marry Alanna! Perhaps we have a chance!"

"Um," Kourrem replied, checking to see that she had threaded the loom properly. "I don't want to be married yet. I have too much to learn."

Alanna laughed outright at this. "And I thought I was the only one who felt that way!"

Ishak returned before the girls left, looking contrite. "I have acted badly," he told Alanna softly. "I will try to slow down. I will listen and do as you say." Overcome with the effort of apologizing to a woman, even if she was the Woman Who Rides Like a Man, he turned and fled. Alanna frowned, wondering if his show of humility was just that—a show. She fingered the ember-stone at her throat and sighed as the clacking of Kourrem's loom began. She could only wait for Ishak's next outbreak and hope that he learned self-control soon.

five

Apprentices

*E*very night Kourrem took time to work on her loom. Even Alanna, who knew nothing of weaving, could see that she spent as much time unraveling mistakes as she did weaving.

"I just don't know enough," she told Alanna one night, as Kara and Ishak argued nearby over the use of a scroll of spells. "I was little when I was taught, and I haven't practiced for a long time." She sighed, looking discouraged. "You remember Hakim Fahrar, the man you fought?" Alanna nodded. "His mother is the best weaver in the tribe. I'd ask her to teach me, but—" She made a face. "The women think Kara and I have forgotten our place because we sit with the men."

"And it doesn't help that I wounded Mistress Fahrar's son," Alanna said shrewdly. Kourrem nodded; Alanna tousled the girl's hair. "I'd give anything to help you, but I don't know how to weave."

All three apprentices—even Ishak—stared at her. Finally Kara whispered, "You don't know how to *weave*?"

"Warriors don't learn such things," Ishak told the girls scornfully.

Kourrem stood abruptly. "I'll be right back." She hurried from the tent.

"I just thought—all the girls are taught when we are very young," Kara explained. "You don't know how to card wool, or spin thread, or—" She stopped, baffled.

"I don't know how to bake, either," Alanna confided. "The only cooking I know is the kind soldiers do on the march."

Kara shook her head. In many ways she was a very proper Bazhir maiden; Alanna often puzzled her. She was trying to explain the process of weaving when Kourrem returned, bearing a lap-sized model of her big loom. The girl knelt beside Alanna. "I can teach you the simplest kind of weaving, if you want to learn," she offered. "You couldn't do anything like stripes, but it would be a start."

"I'd love to learn," Alanna admitted. "It looks like fun." Kourrem grinned. "It is fun when it goes right," she said. "I really shouldn't start you weaving right away. We always had to learn to card wool —you know, comb out all the dirt and tangles— and spin a good thread before we were let *near* a loom."

Alanna laughed. "It's just like every fighting art I studied," she explained to her surprised audience. "We had to learn how to make our weapons before we got to use them."

"You have to understand how a thing is made

before you master it," Kara said wisely. Suddenly her face brightened. "That's what you've been teaching us about magic!"

"So if you know how the crystal sword is made, you can command it!" Ishak added.

Alanna fought down a trace of alarm. "That's not all of it, Ishak." She fixed his eyes with her own grim ones. "To command things of nature, you need to understand how they are made, and you must want to command them. With things of magic, you develop your will until you are stronger than your Gift. Otherwise the power will turn on you. *Do you understand me?*" she demanded.

Ishak met her eyes defiantly, then looked away. "Of course I understand."

Alanna frowned, worried for him, but there was no sense in pursuing the matter now. She examined the loom she held. "What do I do with this thing?"

Kourrem explained the device, naming the different parts and describing what they did. When she finished, she worked the shuttle until a row had grown on the threaded loom. Then she handed it to Alanna. "Your turn."

The loom was clumsy and awkward-feeling to the knight, who was far more used to weapons. At last she drew a breath and started the shuttle.

The moment the thing began to move, she realized she didn't understand what was supposed to be happening. Within seconds the threads were impossibly snarled. Kara choked back laughter;

even Kourrem had to smile. Ishak looked bored.

Alanna put the loom down, feeling younger and more ignorant than she had in years. "Perhaps I need to learn the other things first. My teachers were right—for real skills, there aren't any short-cuts."

"I'll teach you," Kourrem offered, "if you still want to learn. Though it seems silly for you to go to such trouble when the things you do are more important."

"What's more important than the clothes I wear?" Alanna wanted to know.

"Kourrem's right," Ishak remarked scornfully. "Why should you fool with looms and women's things when you can fight and do magic?"

Alanna didn't miss the scorn in Ishak's voice, or that both girls had flushed with embarrassment and begun to finger their veils. *He needs a lesson,* she thought, picking up a thread. *This time I'm going to give him one.* "So you think weaving is stupid?"

"Women's work." Ishak yawned, very much a Bazhir male. "It's all right if you have nothing better to do."

Alanna swiftly tied a knot in the thread. Ishak fell as the carpet he stood on yanked itself out from under his feet, dumping the young man on the ground. The carpet then sailed around the tent frantically. "Did I understand you correctly?" she asked as the girls ducked and Faithful hissed and spit. "Is working with thread less important than talking to demons and seeing the future?"

When Ishak opened his mouth to reply, Alanna swiftly tied a second knot. The carpet stopped its mad journey, coming to a halt directly over Ishak's head. "While I have your attention," Alanna went on, "I'd like to say a few things about thread magic. I've never used it; I learned what I know from our village healing-woman, when I was young, and from the palace Healers. I do know that a woman with a bit of string in her hands can bring down a troop of armed knights, if her will is strong enough. Men—Healers, mostly—use thread magic, too; but women acquire it more easily. I guess that's because most women know how to weave and spin and sew. You owe your fellow apprentices an apology, Ishak."

She loosened the second knot, and the carpet began to lower itself onto Ishak's head. "You can't treat Kara and Kourrem as the men of the tribe treat the women. These women are your equals. What they do—what they learn—is just as important as what you do and learn. Frankly, in some areas they're better at it than you are."

She untied the first knot, and the carpet whisked itself around the tent, stopping in front of Ishak this time. Alanna undid what remained of the second knot, and the carpet trembled. "You're in its way," she told the young man. Startled, he moved aside, and the carpet settled gently into its former spot. "I hope I've made myself clear."

Ishak gasped, his eyes alight with discovery. "Will you teach me how to do that?" he demanded. "I want to learn—women's magic or not!"

A hand painfully squeezed Alanna's heart: for a moment he sounded exactly like her willful brother. "I believe I mentioned an apology."

"I'm sorry," Ishak told the two girls. "I keep forgetting."

Kara was looking at the thread in Alanna's hands with awe. "You mean Kourrem and I could do magic while we are weaving and sewing? Just by making knots?"

Alanna sighed, suddenly feeling tired and old. "I'll teach all of you in the morning," she promised. "For now, let's turn in."

Obedient as always, they left, chattering eagerly. Once they were gone, Faithful jumped onto Alanna's left shoulder (his favorite perching-spot). *That was an interesting display of temper,* he commented. *Why don't you pick on someone who can fight back?*

"He's got to learn," Alanna replied, dousing the lamps. "Otherwise he's going to insult some little old wrinkled lady shaman who will tie *him* in knots."

Perhaps, the cat replied.

"Not just 'perhaps,'" Alanna demurred. "You know as well as I do that there are traps for sorcerers in the strangest places. At least *I* know I mean no harm. Someone else might not be kind."

You won't always be able to stand between another person and his fate, Faithful warned. *You mustn't think you can look after the world.*

Alanna chuckled and tugged her pet's long black tail. "Who will look after it if I don't?"

Faithful gave a disgusted mutter and stuck his cold nose into her ear, surprising a laugh from her.

❧

*T*o the new lessons in knot magic, Alanna added the names and powers of herbs, stones, and metals. Ishak and Kara complained about the added memorization, but they studied hard. Ishak now kept Alanna up at night; he was quicker than the other two, and he had a feel for the Gift, but his eagerness to learn dangerous things frightened her. He did not have the self-discipline of the girls. Was it because he had been more accepted by the tribe? Often Alanna caught him staring at her crystal sword; she feared one day he would ignore her command and try to wield it.

As an apprentice weaver, Alanna was all thumbs; the girls were baffled. She reminded herself that she had not been even a passable swordsman when she first began to train; but such thoughts didn't soothe her hurt pride. Making things worse was the fact that there was no way she could teach Kourrem the advanced skills the girl lacked.

"I can't do it!" Kourrem cried while working one night. A mass of knotted threads, like a giant spider, sat on her loom. "I'm stupid and ignorant—"

"You lost track of the pattern," a dry voice said from the opening that led to the temple part of the tent. Alanna and her apprentices turned to stare at the tiny old woman who stood there. Alanna recognized her. Halef Seif had pointed Hakim's mother out to her before, the woman Kourrem said was the tribe's finest weaver.

The old lady lifted an unlit stick of incense. "I was about to pay my respects to the Mother when I overheard," she explained. Walking forward, she thrust the incense at Alanna. "Hold this." She joined Kourrem at the big loom. "See? Here—and here—you broke the pattern. And here." She inspected the remainder of Kourrem's work as the girl clutched Kara's arm. "Hm. Not bad for someone without much formal teaching. A tight, even weave." Kourrem beamed at the praise. *Perhaps the first she's had from a woman of the tribe in years,* Alanna thought.

Mistress Fahrar walked over and picked up the cards, scrutinizing Alanna's work. "Be more patient," she said, her gray-brown eyes amused. "You're missing little bits of dirt." She thrust the pieces of wool back at Alanna. "Start over, and take your time. You'll be faster as you get accustomed to it."

She drew a breath, looking around her. "You're

a promising weaver, young Kourrem, but you
should be learning your own craft, not teaching it. I
am sure *your* weaving could become better, Kara."
The tall girl blushed and looked at her feet. "And
you should have a teacher who is accustomed to
teaching, shaman," she told Alanna firmly. "You will
learn from me, with Kourrem's permission, and I
will show these two young women what more they
can study. Doubtless this young man can find
something to occupy him while we women work,"
she added dryly.

For the grateful tears and the relief in the girls'
faces, Alanna could have kissed the formidable lady.
Instead she nodded, her face properly grave. "I
accept your kind offer, Mistress Fahrar, for my
apprentices and myself." *At last!* she exulted
inwardly. *One woman in the tribe has acknowledged
that we exist; and I didn't have to ask Halef Seif or
Ali Mukhtab to intervene!*

"I am called Mari," the mother of Hakim
replied. "Now, come, you girls. Show me what else
you can do."

〜

When Coram returned a week later, he found
things very different. He had much to say about the
changes among the Bloody Hawk. Fortunately, he
said all of it in private, to Alanna and Faithful.

"I think I'm leavin' ye in a fairly quiet place," he
began as he unpacked in his tent. Alanna was

watching as she scratched Faithful's ears. "Ye weren't well enough known here that ye could get into any trouble, and I thought they'd stay away from ye. But I come back, and ye're the Mother-blessed shaman of the tribe, ye've adopted three young ones, and ye're forcin' the women to accept two of their own sittin' with the men—"

"You're turning purple," Alanna commented when he stopped for breath.

"Can't ye stay out of trouble for a few short weeks?" he bellowed.

"I didn't ask for Akhnan Ibn Nazzir to attack me," she pointed out. "But he did, and I killed him. I can't leave the tribe without a shaman, can I? Since I have no intention of being killed by the first rival who comes along, or of staying here forever, I picked three apprentices. It's not my fault that two of them are girls; but they are, and the tribe has to treat them with respect if they're ever to be good shamans. And no, I couldn't have chosen just Ishak. What if something happens to him? All three have to be trained anyway, and Bazhir custom—it's easier to break the King's law back home than it is to flout Bazhir custom, have you noticed?—Bazhir custom says *I* have to train them. Besides, having only one shaman when you can have three is silly."

Coram sat heavily and accepted the brandy she poured for him. His broad tanned face was wrinkled with concern. "Lass, ye're settin' these poor folk on their ears," he said wearily. "They haven't changed in centuries, and ye're forcin' them to accept things yer own people can't accept—not easily."

"But don't you see? To the Bazhir, I'm a legend. They take things from me they *wouldn't* take from anyone else. I don't ask them to change for *stupid* reasons. They know having three shamans might make the difference to their survival. Even the women are beginning to accept the girls. At least, Mari Fahrar is."

Coram drained his cup and shook his head when she offered refill. "I'm worried for ye," he confessed. "I hate seein' ye a stranger always. Ye're an odd lass, but ye're like my own kin, and I want ye t'be happy."

Alanna put Faithful down and hugged her friend. "I don't *feel* like a stranger here," she confessed as she wiped her eyes. "It seems to me that I've know these people for a long time—all my life, perhaps. I don't always agree with them, but they make sense to me."

Gruffly, touched by her affection, he asked, "Do ye commune with the Voice of the Tribes at sunset, then? All the way t'the city Hakim made us stop every night while he stared into the fire." He shuddered as he finished unpacking his saddlebags. "'Twas spooky."

Alanna lifted Faithful up again, putting him on her shoulder. "That's one thing I *don't* do," she said ruefully. "It's too much like letting Ali Mukhtab have a part of me. I don't want anyone to have a part of me, not yet, anyway."

"Not even Prince Jonathan?" Coram asked shrewdly. Alanna blushed a deep red, and he chuckled. "He said t'tell ye he'd be seein' ye soon, somethin' about receivin' instruction from Ali Mukhtab. Oh, I've letters for ye, from Lord Thom and Sir Myles." For a moment the burly man struggled with himself; then he gave in. "There's another letter for ye as well." He drew it from beneath his jerkin, handing it to her reluctantly. "I should've burned it when he handed it to me. I'd hoped ye knew better than to still be consortin' with the likes of him."

"George!" Alanna said gleefully. "Is he all right? Has he been—well, safe?"

"He's flourishin', that one," Coram snapped. "And when are ye going t'give over befriendin' a rogue like him?"

Alanna grinned impishly. "When you stop drinking." She laughed as he swore, and returned to read her letters.

George's missive was short, but its contents made her blush. She knew her old friend loved her, and she loved him in a more-than-friendly way, but Jonathan had always been first. George knew it and understood, but his words told her that he continued to hope.

Myles's letter was long and chatty, giving her the news of everyone at Court, nobles and servants. More than any other high-born person Alanna knew, Myles made friends with everyone, not just his social equals. He was able to tell her about Cook and Stefan the hostler with as much detail as he gave to the King and Jonathan. Only when she reread his letter did she notice that he said nothing about Thom.

Thom's own letter more than made up for Myles's omission:

Dear Alanna,

Coram tells me you've been adopted by a bunch of uncivilized desertmen. How odd of you! He tells me now you're a "man of the tribe," which is what you've always wanted, I suppose. No, don't scowl at me.

(Alanna *was* scowling.)

I am enjoying myself here. Everyone is very polite, and the library has some classics of sorcery even my Masters didn't possess. My education grows by leaps and bounds. I have attached some of the late Duke Roger's followers, including the lovely Delia of Eldorne. I have no interest in the lady as such, but I believe she may know where some of Roger's most secret manuscripts are hid. She had hinted as much, and I feel that she doesn't lie.

I enjoy the luxuries: exotic foods, fine clothing, having servants to wait on me. I will travel at some point, but only when there is nothing more to be learned here.

Try not to be too disgusted with me.

Love,
Thom.

∼

Shortly after Coram's return, Mari brought Farda, the tribe's midwife, to make her peace with the new shaman. Within minutes the two were trading secrets of healing. The next day Farda took over instructing the apprentices in herbs: from that moment on, most of the women made their peace with Alanna and her young people. Some would never be won over and would always view the new ways with suspicion, but they were a minority. Knowing to whom she owed the new warmth, Alanna tried to thank Mari Fahrar. The old woman brushed her words aside.

"All things change," she told Alanna frankly. "It does not hurt men to know women have power, too."

Alanna had to laugh. Until Mari and Farda entered her life, she never realized that the tribeswomen viewed their men not with fear but with loving disrespect. Sometimes she felt that *she* was the one getting the education, not her pupils.

Kara was just beginning to work on her control of the wind when the men of the village went hunting for night-raiders: hillmen who carried off a herd of sheep and the boy tending them. Alanna and Coram were teaching the boys archery when the lookouts sounded an alarm.

Coram swore. "They lured the men off a-purpose!" He turned to the boys. "Let's see what yer marksmanship's like on movin' targets."

"What about their shamans?" one woman cried. "They attack first with magic!"

Alanna could feel the unnaturalness of the fierce breeze. "Kara! Kourrem! Ishak!" she yelled, remembering too late they were in Farda's tent, across the breadth of the village. It would cost precious moments to fetch them—

The three apprentices ran up, panting, chasing Faithful. "The cat said the hillmen are attacking and you want us," Ishak gasped. "I don't know how we understood—"

"*I* didn't understand anything," Kourrem pouted. "You and Kara said—"

"Hush!" Alanna ordered. She looked at Coram. "I have to be a shaman—" she began.

The former guardsman was still instructing the boy archers as women and children streamed past them into Alanna's big tent. "Do what ye must do," he said tersely. He grabbed a strong young woman by the arm. "Ye! Grab a spear and stand t'the defense!" She stared at him for a moment, then ran to obey. The older men of the village, those who hadn't been included on the hunt, were already gathering around Coram, accepting his leadership. More women were grabbing spears and axes, leaving their children to the charge of others in the tent.

Alanna led her apprentices to a hill overlooking both the tents and the eastern approaches, from which the now-shrieking winds came. Kara saw the attackers first, hidden behind a wall of dust.

She pointed out five green-robed men astride ponies. "Their shamans wear green, too," she shouted over the wind. "The dust before them is alive. When they came before, Akhnan Ibn Nazzir could not fight them, and the dust devils killed three men."

"I'm not Akhnan Ibn Nazzir!" Alanna shouted back. Drawing the crystal sword, she focused her attention on the length of the blade, holding it directly before her. Now was the time to put its energy to use: it would extend her ability to command things to break and split far more than she could have done normally. She shouted the spell, sending her energy streaking down the smoky blade and into the earth just a few yards in front of the oncoming riders. The earth grumbled and cracked, forming a deep trench. Their own frontal vision ruined by the dust devils, the hillmen in the first rank rode into the trench.

"That'll stop 'em for a minute!" Alanna yelled. "Kourrem, do you have some string?" The girl pulled several hanks of thread from her pocket. She was never without them these days. "Try to hobble as many of their ponies as you can!" Kourrem grinned and started to work, her heavy brows pulled together as she worked.

"Kara!" Alanna continued. "Force the wind back into their faces!" Both girls tore off their veils in order to see more clearly as Alanna turned to her third apprentice. "Ishak—d'you remember how to throw fire?"

"Yes!" he cried.

"When they get close enough, scorch them out of the saddle!"

Ishak bellowed, "What about the dust devils and their shamans?"

"Leave them to me!"

The sound of the high winds changed: Kara was at work, her burnoose whipping frantically around her. The first pony stumbled and fell, thanks to Kourrem, tossing his rider. Flames soared from Ishak's fingers, enveloping a big man.

The hillmen were leaping their ponies over the trench. Once more Alanna pointed the crystal blade and sent her Gift into the ground before the dust devils, breaking it open. The brown columns of dust passed over the second trench as easily as they had the first, and Alanna turned her attention to them, reaching out with her mind to see what they were.

They were mindless blots of energy, wielded by the shamans and collecting desert sand and dirt to give themselves shape. She knew better than to use the sword to split them in two: then she would have twice as many dust devils to contend with. Instead she sent a whip of violet fire at the shamans, determined to end the problem at its source. One dropped to the ground when her magic reached him, screeching in agony. A second streak of fire, red in color, picked off another shaman—Ishak had seen her purpose, and was helping.

Varicolored shields were forming around the remaining three; the element of surprise was gone, and they were defending themselves. Now Alanna called up a sparkling, amethyst-colored wall that encircled one of them, cutting off his air. His pony panicked and reared, dropping him in the dirt as he fought to breathe. When she was sure of his death, Alanna applied the same trick to another shaman. The remaining wizard was already fighting off Ishak's red flame—and losing. With the deaths of the last two, the dust devils collapsed.

Hillmen thundered past them, their numbers reduced. Kourrem sagged and dropped, exhausted from the effort of maintaining five spells at once. Kara was looking white and ill, but with the deaths of the shamans the winds had also stopped. Alanna made her sit down. Ishak was still flaming the raiders, laughing merrily as they tried to put themselves out.

"It's beautiful, Alanna!" he cried loudly, not realizing the winds were gone. "The power is beautiful!"

"Look!" Kara gasped, pointing to the west. Halef Seif and his men were riding furiously into the village, their swords ready. Caught between Ishak, Coram, and the fiercely fighting old men, women, and the boys, as well as the young warriors of the tribe, the hillmen didn't stand a chance.

Alanna picked off those who tried to escape, so that none survived the raid.

The moment the fighting was over, Alanna ushered her apprentices back to the well. Here Farda was already putting women to work cleaning and bandaging wounds. Alanna made Kara and Kourrem sit, then briskly rolled up her sleeves. "Anyone killed?" she asked Farda, washing her hands.

The big midwife shook her head. "Hassam and Mikal are the worst hurt—Hassam with a head wound, Mikal with an open gash on his thigh. Will you see to one?"

Alanna nodded and entered her immense tent, feeling Ishak behind her. The wounded lay quietly on the carpets placed before the plain altar, waiting for someone to see to their hurts. Clearly Farda had taught the women how to care for injuries, because every matron in the village was cheerfully at work. Some of the hurt, such as Hassam, were boys, but they were as silent as the men.

Alanna knelt beside Hassam, smiling at him. A wide-eyed girl, not long a wife, hurried to stand beside her with a basin of hot water and clean bandages. Alanna dipped one in the water, using it to carefully rinse Hassam's wound clean. "What happened to the hillman who gave you this?" she asked jokingly. "Is his spirit looking for a place to rest?"

"Coram cut him down while I fought him," the boy replied, wincing as she gently pulled his hair away from the wound. "He said honor is not necessary when fighting thieves."

"I'll need healing salve, thread, and a very fine needle. Tell Farda," Alanna instructed the waiting girl, who nodded and hurried off. Alanna examined the wound closely. "I think Coram told me the same thing when I was your age—and that wasn't so long ago. Hold still." She closed her eyes and reached out into his body, searching out the full extent of the wound's damage. She grimaced inwardly at the sick feeling in the boy's skull: he had a bad concussion. Still, it could have been far worse: the bone was uncracked, and there was no bleeding in his brain. She squeezed the boy's hand. "You bruised your head," she told him, knowing he would have no idea what "concussion" meant. "You'll be dizzy and sick for a while, and you'll have trouble standing—so don't try it. Now. I'm helping you to sleep so I can sew your wound in peace. All right?" Hassam nodded, his large eyes full of trust. She placed her hands on his once more, reaching for the warm fire of her Gift. This time it flowed softly and peacefully down her arms, making her feel nearly as relaxed as the boy, who went to sleep instantly. She stopped for a moment and sighed, before pulling her mind back to her surroundings. The girl had returned with the materials she needed. Deftly Alanna thrust undyed thread through the needle's eye. Glancing at the watching Ishak, she said, "Make yourself useful, will you? Hold him."

The young Bazhir obeyed, holding the sleeping boy's head gently but firmly between his hands.

"Won't it hurt?" he asked apprehensively as Alanna tested the needle's point.

"Ouch! Not now—not after I've used the Gift to put him to sleep. Steady." Quickly she set her stitches, thanking the gods yet again for the training she had received from the palace Healers during the Tusaine War. The stitches in, she cut the thread and bandaged the wound, using healing salve and a clean bandage. Finally she replaced Ishak's hands with her own. Hassam never stirred. His slumber deepened as she used her Gift again, shoving back the damage done by a hillman's axe. Dimly she could hear Faithful yowling behind her, but her mind was fixed on her work. When she had aided nature all she could, she released Hassam into a real sleep. With luck he would be well soon, with an interesting scar for the maidens to admire.

She stood, her ears roaring. Preoccupied by Hassam's injury, she thought at first she had risen too quickly. Then the sick, weak feeling swelled up from her midsection, and she swore even as her legs buckled. In the excitement of fighting, of keeping control over the crystal sword, of her worry over the tribe's young ones, she had overextended, using more of her Gift than she could afford to give away.

I'll never learn, she thought ruefully as she fainted.

⟋

*I*t was fully dark when she woke. Faithful was howling urgently right into her ear, and a slim hand gripped her shoulder, shaking her. Wearily she opened her eyes, trying to focus without much success. "It's really better if you let me rest," she muttered. "I just overdid a little, that's all."

"Faithful says to wake you," Kara apologized. "He says it's Ishak."

A bolt of alarm shot through Alanna, and she fought to sit up. Bone-deep weariness tugged at her like chains, trying to drag her down. "Ishak? Bless him, what's he doing now?" Her alarm was even greater when she realized that the ember at her neck was warm—no, *hot*.

He has the sword, Faithful cried. *While the tribe met with the Voice, he came here and took the sword!*

Her heart thudding sickly, Alanna lurched to her feet. Her head spun. She held it, forcing her eyes to remain open. She was in no shape for a showdown. Gripping the ember-stone, she sent a plea to the Goddess, for Ishak's sake. Strength washed into her, steadying her shaking limbs.

Closing her eyes, she reached out, searching for a sign—any sign—of her wayward apprentice. Her mind touched the web of magic that was the crystal sword as it vibrated with new heights of fury. The weapon had come to accept her commands, just barely, but it would never accept Ishak. Opening her eyes, she raced toward the hill where they had faced the raiders that morning.

He was shining in his own red fire, the sheathed sword in his hand. An orange glow surrounded the weapon, battling with the young man's magic.

For a second Alanna's mind flickered, and Ishak was replaced by a vision:

An azure sky rapidly clouded over with thunderheads. A pole thrust against it like a pointing finger. At its base a fire burned, and the woman tied to the pole screamed in agony.

The vision was gone, and she could see her apprentice clearly once more. "Ishak! No!" Alanna yelled hoarsely. She reached out, but the bolt of power she threw at him was thin, and it vanished far short of the mark. She would never reach him in time. "Don't! The sword—it'll turn on you!"

"Why should you have it, Woman Who Rides Like a Man?" he yelled back, triumphant. "You won't even use it! You don't use your own Gift as much as you could. You don't deserve to have more! *I* deserve the sword! I want the power!"

"Then why didn't the sword come to you, instead of me?" Alanna cried, hoping to keep him talking. She was at the hill's base now. "You can't use this power, Ishak—the sword's been warped! *No!*"

Ishak drew the sword, holding it aloft. Orange fire shimmered around the shining gray of the blade, pulsing fiercely. He laughed and pointed the sword at Alanna, speaking a word she couldn't hear.

Instinctively she threw all the strength the Goddess had just given her into a shield. She had wanted only to defend herself, but the sword's magic reflected back from her protection, enveloping Ishak in a ball of flame. He screamed, once. Then he was gone.

Tears streaming down her cheeks, Alanna trudged up the hill. There was nothing left of Ishak or of the scabbard he had carelessly thrown on the ground. Wiping her eyes on her sleeve, she wished he could have listened to her just one more time.

The tribespeople were waiting for her when she descended, with the crystal blade shimmering in her hand. "What will you do now?" Halef Seif inquired softly.

"I'm going to finish training your two shamans, that's what I'm going to do," she replied grimly. "What else is there?"

six

Ceremonies

The first of the Bazhir shamans arrived a week after Ishak's fatal mistake with the crystal blade. They came sometime during the night; when Alanna arose in the morning, they were seated cross-legged before the altar. Faithful sat facing them, blinking solemnly as he returned their stares.

They told Alanna they had come to teach and to learn, that every wise shaman tried to study new things. They meant what they said, and they were not alone. Within days more arrived with their apprentices until—with Alanna, Kara, and Kourrem—fourteen shamans and six apprentices were trading spells in the tents of the Bloody Hawk.

"You should be pleased," Ali Mukhtab remarked one night as he and Alanna sat up late. "You have done more than most Bazhir have accomplished in a lifetime. You have made girls shamans. You have begun a school for magic that will live and grow to become the greatest such school in existence. Even priests from the City of the Gods will come, even the warrior-sorcerers of Carthak."

Alanna stared at the Voice of the Tribes. He had that misty, far-seeing look in his dark eyes that privately gave her the crawls. "You *knew* this school was going to happen?" she gasped. "And you never said anything?"

He smiled and puffed on his long-stemmed pipe. "I have learned—as all who would become the Voice must learn—to keep my silence about the future. It will happen without my help."

Alanna snorted, and thought about it for long silent moments. At last she pointed out, "I still haven't gotten Kara and Kourrem to leave off their face veils." She didn't discuss it with the girls any longer because it was a subject they could not agree on.

"They are right," Mukhtab pointed out. "They have overcome too many old ideas, but this one they can never change. A woman without a veil is a woman of bad repute among the tribes. Good women may not speak to her, and good men may not know her."

Alanna thought of the women of the Court of the Rogue and sighed. "That's sad. Some of the most intelligent women I knew as I was growing up were prostitutes. I didn't know many noble ladies well, you see." Suddenly the ground beneath her trembled, and she looked up. "Visitors? At this hour?"

Grinning, Mukhtab knocked the ashes from his pipe into the fire. "I think you will like these visitors."

They emerged from the tent to find the tribesmen gathered around the newcomers. These were
five: two riders from the tribe, a man-at-arms in
Barony Olau colors, and—to Alanna's joy—Myles
of Olau and Prince Jonathan.

✑

Somehow she greeted the guests and introduced
them to the headman, the Voice, the visiting
shamans, and the apprentices. Jonathan captivated
Kourrem, while Kara watched Myles with awe-
widened eyes. Once the knight smiled at her, saying, "There's a dancing bear in Corus who's almost
as shaggy as I am." Kara blushed beneath her veil
and fled.

The noblemen greeted Alanna and Coram with
warmth, reaching across carefully maintained dis-
tances to shake hands.

A guest-tent was prepared for the newcomers;
but somehow, when it came time to retire, the
Prince followed Alanna to her home. Once inside
the tent, they were alone—even Faithful had found
someplace else to be.

For long moments they stared at each other: the
short, red-headed, violet-eyed woman in a Bazhir's
pale blue robe, its hood thrust back from her hair,
and the tall, broad-shouldered young man, his hair
coal-black, his eyes a brilliant sapphire blue. He
wore serviceable tan breeches and a cotton shirt
beneath a tunic of his favorite royal blue, but only a
blind man would not have seen his royal heritage.

"I didn't want to disgrace you in front of the tribesmen," he said at last, his deep voice making her shiver happily. "Myles said women don't touch men in public."

"No," she replied, twisting her hands in her robe.

Awkward, he tried again. "I'm going to be here for a while. Ali Mukhtab says there's much I have to learn."

"Do their Majesties know where you are?"

He shrugged. "They know I'm with Myles. I told them I had to get away from the court. I'm tired of people fawning all over me." He smiled. "No one argues with me, now that you're gone."

Troubled by the arrogant tone of his voice and the flash of pride in his eyes, she asked, "Is that the only reason you came? To get away from home?"

"Of course not." Suddenly he swore. Covering the space between them in two great strides, he seized her and held her tight, burying his face in her shoulder. Alanna threw her arms around his neck. *This* was the Jonathan she loved.

He forced her to look at him. "I missed you so much," he whispered. He kissed her fiercely. She returned the kiss, feeling heat rush through her at his touch. He bore down to her sleeping mat; in the time that followed, they knew they still desired each other.

Afterward, Alanna got up to blow out the lamps. He watched her as she moved around the tent. "What are you grinning about?" he wanted to know as she doused the last light.

She lay down and snuggled up against his shoulder, smiling contentedly. "Well, 'women of bad reputation' go without veils among the Bazhir," she confided. "All this time I haven't worn a veil, but it took me until tonight to get a bad reputation."

Jon chuckled and kissed her. "I'm glad to hear that. I was worried about you, among all these handsome men."

"You didn't have to," she grinned. "They respect me as a shaman and a warrior, but they don't even remember I'm a woman most of the time."

"Silly of them," Jonathan whispered. "I can't forget it—not that I haven't tried, these past months."

"I'm sure you have," Alanna drawled, remembering how the women of the Tortallan Court always flocked around her Prince.

For a while they were silent in the dark, thinking, and being content just to hold each other. Then Alanna ventured, "Jon?"

"I intend to become the Voice of the Tribes." He stroked her hair.

Alanna sat up. "How did you know that was what I wanted to ask?"

She could feel his shrug. "I just did."

Slowly she lay back down. "Ali Mukhtab said the ceremony is dangerous."

"I need the power I can get from it. The Bazhir are incredible people, Alanna. Their history is as old as ours—older. And we lose too many men to the Bazhir. It will be better for everyone if they take part in Tortall, instead of tying up our armies within our own borders."

"I've been happy among them," she admitted. "I'll be glad when they aren't at war with our soldiers."

"Have you been so content that you won't consider leaving?"

Alanna stiffened, feeling wary. "I have to bring Kara and Kourrem through the Rite of Shamans before I can go. Why?"

"Once that's done, I had hoped you would come home."

"I doubt that the scandal over my fight with Duke Roger has died down," she reminded him.

He silenced her with a hand over her lips. "Come as my betrothed."

The word lay between them, growing larger and larger. Finally Alanna gasped, "Jon, I can't."

"Why not?"

"Because I'm a scandal. I killed your cousin. For six years I was disguised as a boy—"

"*I* knew what you were, for most of that time."

"You should marry a princess who'll bring you power and gold," she went on. "That's your duty. And you should marry a virgin."

"You were a virgin when we first made love."

"No one *else* knows that!" she cried, frustrated. Remembering the tent's thin walls, she lowered her voice. "They'll say I was in bed with a whole regiment, behind your back."

"Do you think your friends will permit that kind of talk? You have more friends at Court than you know. As to my marrying someone who will bring me power—what of you? You're a woman knight and a Bazhir shaman. I could marry the daughter of a Bazhir chief, and not gain as much stature as I will if I marry you. Besides," he went on, his voice suddenly hard, "I'm tired of worrying about such things. I want what *I* want, not just what's good for Tortall. I've spent my entire life watching what I say and do, for fear of upsetting the merchants, or the Gallans, or the priests, or *anyone*. *They* should worry about upsetting *me*— not the other way around!"

"Is that why you're asking *me* to marry you?" she whispered. "Because you want to prove to everyone you don't care?"

For a long moment he didn't reply. When he spoke, his voice was very low. "I thought you loved me, Alanna."

"I do!" she whispered fiercely. "I do! But—" What he had said—the resentment in his voice— worried her. And how could she explain that it was wonderful not to have to trouble herself over Court plots and plotters? Not to have to watch how she acted or what she said, apart from not offending her new tribe? For the first time she could be fully and completely Alanna; she was still learning just who "Alanna" was.

"Marry me, sweet one," he whispered. "I love you. I want you for my wife."

It was too much, all at once. "Let me think about it," she begged. "I *do* love you, Jon. I just need time."

"All right." His voice sounded amused. As they went to sleep, Alanna wondered, *Just what is so funny?*

∾

*A*s usual, she rose with the dawn. Jon continued to sleep. She dressed quietly and went into the temple portion of her tent. Myles was already there, looking as fresh as he ever did in the morning. Alanna hugged her old friend tightly, and together they walked out into the sunlight. She showed him the village, even taking him up to the hill where she had faced the hillmen with her apprentices, and where Ishak had met his doom. She said nothing about Jonathan's proposal, half-hoping that if no one mentioned it, Jon might reconsider.

"Why did you come?" she asked as they climbed down the hill.

"I thought it might be better for Jonathan if someone bore him company."

"You're always so sensible." Alanna grinned. She waved to Mari, who was opening the sides of her tent to the morning air. "Mari Fahrar," she explained to Myles. "She's the best weaver in the tribe. She's teaching me."

Myles chuckled, his green-brown eyes dancing with amusement. "Women's work, Sir Knight?"

Alanna blushed deeply. "I don't want to be ignorant."

Myles hugged her around the shoulders. "You're brave, to admit you don't know everything and then do something about it."

"That's all very well, but I'm a terrible weaver."

"I am told practice helps," he said, his eyes still amused. "Alanna, I actually came here for two reasons."

"Oh? You're keeping Jon company—what's the second one?"

Myles tugged his beard thoughtfully. "I've been thinking about your situation, now that Thom is at Court and you are roaming." He put his hand on her shoulders. "I believe you know I have always been very fond of you."

She smiled. "You're the only one I know who's forgiven me for lying about what I really am."

"I knew long before you told me, remember. Listen to me now. Thom lives well at Court—"

"He's entitled," Alanna pointed out, bristling in her brother's defense. "He *is* the Lord of Trebond. He lived like a priest for years."

"I don't question his right to do so. I *am* concerned about you. If you continue to travel, you will need funds, to stay at inns, to give bribes—don't frown. Some nations use the bribe to support the national treasury. Now, consider *my* problem: I'm not getting any younger; I'm unwed and unsociable. It's not likely that I shall marry and have children. *You've* been like a daughter to me—sometimes even like a son." His eyes twinkled. "I want to make you my heir."

Alanna opened her mouth to reply, but no sound emerged. Her throat felt tight and closed; her eyes burned with tears. He clapped her on the shoulders and let her go. "No need to answer right away."

"I can't refuse," she whispered, hugging him fiercely. "Myles, how do I thank you?"

He tousled her hair. "Nonsense. *I* get an heir who knows how to manage an estate, after all the time you ran Trebond for your brother."

"With Coram's help," she reminded him.

"With Coram's help, but you made the big decisions. And I know you'll care for Barony Olau as I do." He rubbed his hands together. "Now that's decided, what about some food?"

∾

*A*lanna was washing up after breakfast when Farda sought her out. "I wish to speak with you privately, and I believe you will be needed elsewhere when I am finished."

Alanna told Umar Komm, the oldest and most

respected of the shamans, who now ran their "school." He nodded, and she left her tent, which was filled with visiting shamans, apprentices, Jonathan, and Myles. Farda took her to her own home, pressing a cup of tea on the knight.

"It is the Voice of the Tribes," she said abruptly, her plain face worried. "He is ill. My knowledge is not great enough that I can tell what is wrong, but he is sick, I know. He had me promise to say nothing to you before, but I cannot remain silent."

Alanna frowned. She *thought* Ali Mukhtab had looked pale when she encountered him lately, but such meetings had always occurred at night: she had been blaming flickering torch- and firelight. "I'll need my healer's bag," she murmured. Farda handed it to her silently; she must have gotten it from one of the girls. "Why did you come to me? Surely one of the visiting shamans—"

Farda drew herself up, insulted. "You are the shaman for the Bloody Hawk. Do I tell all those guests that our shaman is not good enough for the Voice of the Tribes?"

Alanna grinned. "Sorry I asked."

Ali Mukhtab grimaced as she entered his tent. "No woman, not even Farda, can keep silent," he grumbled. He was pale and sweating as he reclined on his bed.

Alanna knelt beside him and opened the cloth bag in which she kept her healing materials. "Farda did the right thing. Hush."

The examination was brief. All she had to do was reach into him with her Gift. Death was there—black, ugly, and ravaging—rooted in his chest. She sat back on her heels, her own face as white as his. "You've known about this for a while," she accused. "There's no way you could not have known."

"It is given to the Voice to see his ending," he agreed.

"Why did you let it go?" she demanded, sick at heart. She *liked* Ali Mukhtab. "Any raw shaman could have slain it at the start—"

"It is my time," the Voice replied tiredly. "I will not fight it."

"If you had, you'd be healthy today."

He smiled. "Poor Woman Who Rides Like a Man. You know so much, and nothing at all."

"I can do little now," she told him quietly. "The illness is too far along." She took his hand, his image blurred by tears. "I'm sorry, Ali Mukhtab."

He squeezed her hand in reply. "Can you help me with the pain? I must teach Prince Jonathan our laws."

She nodded. Slowly she reached out with her Gift, its violet fire streaming into his body through their combined hands.

The wrinkles smoothed out of the Voice's face, and he slept. Shaking her head to clear it, Alanna busied herself mixing herbs into a small jar. She looked up at Farda. "When he wakes, give him tea made with just a pinch of this," she whispered. "No more than that—it's very strong. And each morning he'll need me for the spell."

Farda stopped her as she made for the door. "How much longer?" the midwife asked, her dark eyes large with hurt.

Alanna shrugged, feeling tired and overburdened. "If I don't do anything unnatural, he has another month," she said bluntly. She walked into the bright sunshine. If anyone saw her wiping her streaming eyes, she could blame it on the light.

∽

The new guests began to arrive within days of Jonathan's coming. These visitors were headmen and leaders of the Bazhir, the lawmakers and the law enforcers. It was clear to everyone that they had come to look over the man who proposed to be the Voice, and it was equally clear they were unhappy with what they saw: the son of the hated Northern King, who was not a Bazhir.

Real trouble did not begin until Amman Kemail, headman of the Sunset Dragon tribe, joined them. Alanna noticed him following Jonathan and Ali Mukhtab during the day, and her instincts for such things warned her of trouble. She recognized the considering look in Kemail's eyes as he listened to Jonathan answering Mukhtab on points of Bazhir law: as if the Bazhir were weighing the Prince and finding him wanting. Still less did she like the way other men drew Kemail aside to talk to him. This tall, brawny headman was clearly a leader, and his appearance was causing many other Bazhir to unburden themselves of their doubts about Ali Mukhtab's choice.

"There's going to be trouble," Alanna told Jonathan as they washed up for the evening meal. "Amman Kemail. I'd bet on it."

Jon drew himself up, clearly offended. "Are you hinting that I can't take care of myself? I'll thank you to remember that I was a knight when you were still a squire—*my* squire!"

"What is the matter with you these days?" Alanna cried, exasperated. "Excuse me very much, Your Royal Highness! I wasn't aware I was questioning your skill in the manly art of self defense; I was silly enough to worry you might get hurt! Forgive me! Permit Your Highness's humble servant to remind you that these people play for keeps!" She hurled down her towel and marched outside, clenching her jaw until it hurt. Jon had been sharp-edged since his arrival, almost as if he had to prove something to himself, or to her. She didn't like it. At the palace, the only thing it seemed necessary to prove was mutual passion. *That* part of their love remained; but sometimes now when he talked, she wanted to cover her ears and shut out his voice.

Which of us has changed? she wondered as she sat down among the Bazhir men. *And in the Mother's Name, why?*

A moment or two later Jonathan took his seat beside Ali Mukhtab. He looked at Alanna and smiled, shaking his head. *As if I were a willful child who'd thrown a very small tantrum,* she told herself. She looked down at Faithful, who was settling himself before her. The cat's tail was twitching madly. He expected trouble as much as Alanna did.

Amman Kemail waited until the women began to pass the food. Ali Mukhtab was offering a piece of his bread to Jonathan when the Sunset Dragon headman stood, pointing at the Prince.

"I will not break bread with the son of the Northern King!"

What little talk there was died out completely. Myles, sitting beside Alanna, whispered, "I should have guessed."

Slowly Ali Mukhtab glanced up at the standing man. "Have you a complaint to voice, Amman Kemail?"

"He is not one of us. He has not won the right to sit with us in peace, or to take bread from the hand of the Voice of the Tribes. Let him prove himself before us all, in the combat!"

"The combat has been demanded of Jonathan, who is the son of the Northern King," Ali Mukhtab said tonelessly. "Who will speak against it?"

Before Alanna could rise to her feet, Kara and Kourrem gripped her shoulders, and Faithful jumped on her lap.

"Think!" Myles hissed, talking fast. "He's not

accepted by them even as a warrior, let alone as the Voice. If you interfere, they will always wonder if he lets others do his fighting. He was a full knight during the war with Tusaine—he's no unblooded boy!"

"He's never fought hand-to-hand, outside the palace courtyards!" Alanna whispered, shaking.

"But George Cooper taught him as well as he taught you! Exercise your common sense, Alanna!"

She knew Myles was right. That didn't help her as she watched Jon prepare. He stripped off his tunic, shirt, and boots, his face pale and set. Coram held his knife while he began his loosening-up exercises. Amman Kemail was also stripping down to his loincloth, his dark face set. Muscle for muscle he and Jon were equally matched, although the Bazhir was a few inches taller.

Alanna shook off Kara and Kourrem and went to crouch by the Prince. "Think about what you want to accomplish here," she whispered, forgetting their quarrel earlier. "The Bazhir are strict when it comes to their honor. Don't shame Kemail."

He grinned up at her. "What about shaming myself?"

She smiled back. "You've yet to do that, Prince. Pardon my suggesting it, but perhaps now is *not* the time to start."

He grabbed her hand and kissed it. "You worry too much, Lady Alanna." Standing, he accepted his knife from Coram with a nod of thanks. Both men were ready, and Ali Mukhtab gave the signal to begin.

Amman Kemail lunged forward, his knife drawing a bloody gash down Jonathan's chest. The Prince faltered back, and the Bazhir lunged again. Alanna closed her eyes. There was a rumble of amazement, and she looked. Kemail's left arm hung uselessly, blood dripping from the wound in his shoulder, and Jonathan was crouched and circling.

The Bazhir charged forward, and Alanna blinked. Jonathan lunged back, then forward again; his left foot connected solidly with Kemail's chest. The Bazhir fell to the ground with a crash. Weakly he struggled to his feet just as Jon lunged for him again. His right fist, weighted with his dagger hilt, lashed forward in another movement too quick for Alanna to follow, striking Kemail squarely on the chin. The Bazhir dropped and lay still, knocked unconscious.

Ali Mukhtab came forward. "He is yours to kill," the Voice commented, his face revealing none of his feelings. Around them the Bazhir men, guests and the Bloody Hawk alike, were silent. "You have won. It is your right."

Jonathan shook his head. "Amman Kemail was honest in expressing his doubts. Were I in his place, I would have done the same. I can't kill a man for not liking me, although I can hope he will change his mind when he knows me better."

Men came forward and carried the still-unconscious headman out of the circle, back to his own tent. Those who remained watched Jonathan thoughtfully.

Coram rushed forward with a drying-cloth, and Kara handed Alanna her healer's bag. She started to work on Jonathan's chest wound: the blood from it was already clotting. "How did I do?" Jon said, panting, accepting a skin of water from Kourrem.

"Where did you learn that kind of fighting: kicking, and that style of punching?" she demanded, rubbing salve into the gash. "George never taught you to fight like that."

Jonathan smiled at her. "About a month after you left, a Shang warrior called The Wolf came to stay at the palace. I've been studying with him. I just never thought what he taught me would be useful so soon."

"Shang warriors are tricky," Coram admitted. "But this one did well by ye."

"What's a Shang warrior?" Kara whispered to Alanna.

"They're trained to fight from childhood," Myles answered. "They can handle all manner of weapons as if born holding them, but they're deadliest with their bare hands and feet. The men and women—"

"And *women?*" gasped Kourrem, surprised.

"Not many women survive the Shang way of life, but those who do are as legendary as the men," Myles replied. "As I was saying, they set great store by personal honor and skill, always seeking new challenges and never staying long in one place."

"Like Alanna," Kara pointed out.

"Very like," Myles agreed, smiling slightly.

Alanna finished bandaging the Prince. It was funny to hear Myles teaching the girls much as he had taught her. She stitched the bandage closed as Ali Mukhtab came over to them.

"You have earned your way among the Bazhir, Jonathan of Conté," he said formally. "Will you join with our people now?"

Jonathan nodded, standing. "What must I do?"

Alanna, Myles, and the others watched as Jonathan underwent the ceremony that bound him to the Bazhir and the desert. Only a fool would not have noticed that the Bazhir were less happy with Jonathan's becoming a Bazhir than the men of the Bloody Hawk had been when Alanna had joined them. They were quiet as Ali Mukhtab cut Jon's arm and his own, and there was no feast afterward.

"They welcomed you, didn't they?" Jon asked Alanna when they were in bed.

"Yes," she whispered.

"They're still not convinced I'll be a good Voice of the Tribes. I'll simply have to prove it with my actions," he commented. He hugged Alanna close. "I know I've been a bit difficult to be around lately," he confessed. "I've been hemmed in and proper all my life, and lately it's been bothering me. I want to break loose and do all the things I'm not supposed to. I'll probably never do them, and right now I'm fighting it. Can you understand that?"

"No," Alanna replied frankly. "I've spent all my life trying to avoid getting caught in just that kind of trap."

"Well, my lovely Lioness, that's the trap I was born into. I'll get over this restlessness, I suppose. I really do want to be a good king, and a good Voice of the Tribes."

"Then you'll do it," she reassured him. "I don't doubt it for a minute."

∾

After Jonathan's initiation into the Bazhir, Alanna spent little time with Kara and Kourrem, leaving them to study with the visiting shamans. Her visits to Ali Mukhtab grew to twice a day, leaving her weary and sick each time. Only Farda and the Voice himself knew what she was doing. During her free hours, she talked with Myles, learning all she needed to know about Barony Olau, even as Jon studied late with Mukhtab.

At last Myles admitted that Alanna had nothing left to learn about his estates. "If you don't mind, I'd like to formally adopt you here. The Bazhir ceremony is simple, and quite legal." He chuckled. "I think your desert friends would be happy if you gained a father, even a disreputable one like me."

Alanna hugged him. She was discovering that each time she hugged Myles, it got easier. It was one of the many ways in which living as a girl was far more pleasant; boys were not supposed to show affection openly. "You aren't disreputable at all; well, not *that* disreputable. If only you'd wear nicer clothes. It's not as if you can't afford it." She had discovered Myles was far wealthier than she dreamed, as a result of an unnoble-like interest in trade.

"But I'm comfortable this way," the knight pointed out. He added shrewdly, "Of course, if you married Jon, I would have to dress up from time to time."

Faithful uttered a small yowlp as Alanna stared at her friend. "How did you know?"

"I'm not blind. All the way down here he was brooding. When he wasn't, he talked about why a Prince marries."

"Oh." Alanna fingered her ember-stone. "I told him I'd think about it."

"Why?"

"I'm not sure he wants to marry me for the right reasons," she admitted. "He seems angry that people expect him to behave a certain way because he's the Prince. He calls it 'a trap' he was 'born into.'" Picking up Faithful, Alanna draped him around her shoulders. "I don't blame him for wanting to rebel—that's one of the reasons *I* left the Court. But I don't like the idea of his proving he's rebelling by marriage with me. That makes me into a thing that's evidence he can do what he wants, instead of leaving me a person."

"He *does* love you," Myles pointed out.

She sighed. "I know he does. But I wonder if he'd have proposed if he weren't—itchy. You know something else, Myles? I never liked people watching me and talking about me all the time, even when they were saying nice things. And I still haven't learned to live with killing Roger." The cat thrust his nose into her ear, and she winced. "I like it here. The Bazhir accept me. I'm myself with them. Well, as much myself as *anyone* can be when they're a shaman and a warrior, and when they don't want to hurt people's feelings."

"Do you love Jon?"

Alanna scratched Faithful's ears, her violet eyes sad. "Love's wonderful, but it is not enough to keep us together for years of marriage. I'm not sure if I'm ready; I'm not sure if Jon's ready. I *have* to be sure, if I want to marry King Roald's heir." She smiled. "Yes, I love him. That's the whole problem."

He stood, putting a hand on her shoulder. "The only advice I can give you, then, is to decide carefully. If you are so uncertain, you would make a bad decision if you married now. No can always be changed to yes, but it's very hard to change yes to no. Come on. Smile. Let's go see what your apprentices are up to."

                         ∾

The apprentices were easy to find. All of the shamans in the village, as well as Jonathan, Ali Mukhtab, Farda, and Halef Seif, were gathered

around the well. In the open space before Ali
Mukhtab's tent stood Kara, her veils whipping
around her as she raised a whirling funnel of dust
in the air before her. Alanna had to grin with pride.
The Bazhir maiden had come a long way from
being unable to control the winds she summoned.

Then Kourrem stepped forward, a bit of thread
in her hands. Her lips moving, she tied a complex
knot in the thread. The twister, which had been
slowly growing toward the sky, halted. Dust fell
slowly down its sides and was scooped in once
more. Kourrem grinned and tied a second, harder
knot: the dust collapsed to earth. The shamans
applauded the two girls, who laughed and blushed
behind their veils.

"They know as much as any shaman," Umar
Komm told Alanna. "They must be initiated soon."

Alanna frowned. "They're very young. If I
leave, I'm afraid they'll get into trouble."

The old man chuckled. "You worry over them
as the desert grouse worries over her chicks," he
informed her. "But you are right. A shaman who is
too young can lead a tribe to grief. I believe
Mahman Fadul would like to be principal shaman
of my tribe." He nodded to the young man who
had come with him, a handsome fellow who
had a habit of watching Alanna with admiration.
"If you wish, I will come to the Bloody Hawk and
watch over your chicks, Woman Who Rides Like a
Man. I can oversee this school of shamans while the

young ones tend to the needs of the tribe."

Alanna nibbled her thumb. "I guess I'm worried that I'd be deserting *my* post," she admitted.

Umar Komm shook his head. "No one believes you will remain among us all your life. That you have stayed so long is an honor to our people. And you may always return."

Alanna felt as if a heavy burden had been lifted from her shoulders. "If that is so, then I gladly accept your offer," she said. "The full moon is in five days—the girls can be initiated then."

"Excellent." Umar Komm nodded. "I shall tell the women of the tribe to prepare a feast we will long remember." He was silent for a moment, then he drew her aside. "Alanna, how ill is the Voice of the Tribes?"

Alanna glanced at Ali Mukhtab. He was leaning on a tall staff, his face grayish under his tan. "Why do you ask?"

"The shamans speak of it quietly, among themselves. We have eyes and can see. He is dying, is he not?"

Alanna nodded.

"Our people begin to suspect. When we commune with the Voice, he *feels* old. And tired. His mind is a disciplined one, and he lets nothing else through, but had you touched his thoughts when he was in his prime—"

"I've never communed with the Voice," she admitted.

Umar Komm smiled. "Of course not. You are afraid you will lose yourself if you join with another—even if you join only in love, as with your Northern Prince."

"Does *everyone* know my business?" she demanded tartly, just remembering to keep her voice down.

"The Bazhir have clear eyes," the shaman replied. "And the lords from the North both love you, each in his own way. It would be a fine thing for our people if the Woman Who Rides Like a Man were to wed the Voice of the Tribes."

"And if I don't?" she asked steadily.

His face was surprised. "Why, then you are still the Woman Who Rides Like a Man, and he is still the Voice. *If* he passes the rite, of course."

Alanna excused herself, seeing that Ali Mukhtab needed to go inside and lie down. "*If,*" *indeed,* she thought.

∽

*T*hat night, after the evening meal, Halef Seif took her aside. "Sir Myles of Olau tells me he wishes to bring you into his tent as his heir," he said. Alanna nodded, and a smile brightened the headman's face. "I feel strange saying he wishes you to be his daughter, since a daughter cannot inherit all the father owns among our people. He says to me you have been friends a long time."

"He taught me everything I knew about the

Bazhir before I came here," she said. "In fact, he taught me a number of useful things when I was growing up. I'm honored that he wants to adopt me."

"Many strange things have happened to you since your birth," Halef mused. "I believe finding a father when you are grown is no stranger than any. Do you wish the ceremony to be done tonight?"

"*Tonight?*"

"Why delay? You have your tribe around you, your Prince to give his blessing—"

Alanna swallowed the lump that had formed in her throat. "Why not tonight, indeed?" she said bravely. "Uh—will this be like the time I was adopted into the tribe?"

"Exactly like," he admitted as he ushered her back into the circle of firelight. Alanna looked at the scar on her wrist from her initiation into the tribe and grimaced. She was vain enough not to want any more scars than she had, but sensible enough to know she would probably collect more in the life she had chosen. Halef Seif was holding up his hands, calling for everyone's attention. Myles stood, dusting off the back of his breeches.

"Tonight the northerner called Myles of Olau, the Friend of the Bazhir, desires to take Alanna of the Bloody Hawk into his tent as his daughter and heir." He waited for the surprised murmurs to end before speaking again. "By our law, seven men must witness this rite. Who will witness?"

Alanna blushed as nearly every man in the circle volunteered. Halef Seif picked Ali Mukhtab, Jonathan, Coram, Umar Komm, Gammal the smith—

"Halef Seif," Alanna said nervously. The headman looked at her. "I would like my apprentices to witness."

Again there was a murmur; women were not legally permitted to perform in ceremonies such as this. Alanna clenched her teeth. If they were to be shamans, the girls would have to take part in every tribal activity. Kara and Kourrem hung back, but the men urged them forward until they stood with the other witnesses. Halef Seif was heating his knife blade in the big fire.

"Roll up your sleeve and smile," Myles whispered as he did the same. Alanna rolled up her right sleeve, thinking that it was not the same as receiving a wound in battle: on those occasions it was often long moments before she even knew she was hurt, and the excitement of fighting acted as its own pain-killing drug. Now she could only brace herself as Halef Seif lightly cut Myles's wrist, then hers, pressing them together as blood welled out. Once again Alanna felt odd joining-magic as Halef Seif commanded, "Become one with each other, with the Bazhir, with the desert we love." The combined drops fell, soaking into the sand as the tribesmen cheered.

"Now, was that so bad?" Myles asked her as

Farda bandaged them both. Alanna grimaced and watched the witnesses sign the legal documents Myles had brought with him from Corus. Then she realized she now had a father who loved her, and she laughed as tears ran down her face.

∾

Jonathan found her later as she struggled once more with the crystal blade, forcing another spot of evil out of the sword's makeup. She smiled up at him as he wiped sweat from her forehead with a cool cloth. "I think that every time I do this, my Gift gets stronger," she gasped.

He frowned at her. "Does it always tire you so much?" When she didn't answer, he added softly, "Or does it tire you because you're wearing yourself out keeping Ali Mukhtab alive?"

"I have to do it, if you're to become the Voice," she replied, turning the sword over in her fingers. "That's what you want—and that's what he wants. I think you could probably handle this, now." She offered it to him. "It's not as bad as it was when I took it from Ibn Nazzir."

He took the weapon, his eyebrows lifting as he felt its power. "It must have been terrible."

She shrugged. "I just wish I knew how it was related to Duke Roger."

He returned the sword, hilt-first, and she sheathed it. "I was asking Myles about that. He reminded me of something—did you know that

Roger was a famous amateur jeweler when he was younger?"

She stared at him, eyes wide. "No."

"He made hilts, pendants—I think he designed his sorcerer's rod. I believe the hilt for this sword is his work."

"And the blade?" she wanted to know.

He smiled grimly. "I've been going through Roger's books and papers, those I can find. I know more about him than I did when he died. Yes, my love, I believe that blade is his work too. I wish you were carrying Lightning again."

"I do, too. I'll just have to keep searching for a way to mend it." She sighed, then put the sword down and let him give her a hand up from the pillow on which she sat. She had been working before the altar; now he led her back to the sleeping quarters.

"Alanna?" he asked as she prepared for the night. "Do you still wear that charm Mistress Cooper gave you to keep you from getting pregnant?"

She showed it to him, hanging half-hidden on the same chain that suspended her ember-stone. "I never go without it."

"I trust you'll leave it off after we're married," he said with a yawn.

I don't want to have children just yet! she realized in a panic. Controlling her emotions, she replied dryly, "We're not married yet, my Prince."

He chuckled sleepily. "Of course not, my beautiful Lioness. Come to bed."

～

*T*he day before the moon was full, Alanna roused Kara and Kourrem before dawn. She rode with them as their sole escort to the nearest oasis. After saying prayers over them, she sent the girls into the chilly water for the ritual cleansing. They were silent throughout. Neither of them was permitted to speak until the night's ritual was over. Neither could use magic, or perform any tasks apart from dressing. Silently they returned to the camp and to Alanna's tent, where they knelt before the altar. Two pairs of eyes fixed on the lamp that burned there; within moments they were in a light trance. They would remain like this for hours, thinking about the life they were about to begin.

The sun was rising when she entered Ali Mukhtab's tent. The Voice was already awake, accepting a cup of tea from Farda.

"And so your chicks have begun the ritual." Alanna made a face as she opened her healer's bag; Umar Komm's description of her apprentices was now known to the entire tribe. "How does that make you feel?"

"As if I were taking the Ordeal of Knighthood all over again," she admitted, feeling for his heartbeat in his wrist. "How did you sleep?"

"Do you expect me to say I slept as an infant

does?" His sense of humor twinkled out of his too-large eyes. His weight loss was now apparent to even the least observant members of the tribe, as was the grayish tinge of his skin.

"I expect you to do me the credit of not lying about it." She placed both hands on his arm and drew a breath, readying herself to beat back the pain once more. Each time it got harder, for her and for him.

When she released him, she rocked backward and would have fallen if Farda had not caught her. She felt dizzy and sick; it was the way she always felt when she used the spell now, and she used it three times a day. She accepted the cloth Farda gave her and wiped her forehead. Already Mukhtab's eyelids were drooping.

"How much longer must Jonathan study?" she rasped, her voice as sick as the rest of her. "When will he be ready?"

She had to place her ear by the dying man's mouth to hear what he was saying. "In the dark of the moon. Fourteen days."

"What if he fails?" The thought was horrible: if he failed, Jon would be dead, and Ali Mukhtab—

The Voice struggled to smile. "Then I will wait to die. Alanna—"

"Yes?"

"Akhnan Ibn Nazzir survived the rite of shamans. Your chicks will do well."

The light of the full moon turned the desert

sands an eerie white: *A fit setting for an initiation, I suppose,* Alanna thought as Umar Komm read the list of gods given honor by the Bazhir. The girls knelt in the sand, encircled by witch-fires that glowed Alanna's violet and Umar Komm's blue-green. Both apprentices looked tired but serene, and Alanna felt proud of them. *They'll be good for the tribe,* she realized, *even if they do want to keep their face veils.*

Umar Komm finished the names of the gods and nodded to Alanna. She stretched out her hands to the girls, conscious that everyone who had come to the tents of the Bloody Hawk in recent days was watching. The circle of fire lay solidly between Alanna and her apprentices. "If you are pure in heart and strong of will, come forth!" she summoned, using words Umar Komm and the other shamans had taught her that very day.

Kara stood. For a moment she faltered, seeing the magical flames rear higher than her head. Then her mouth firmed, and she walked through the ring. Kourrem followed without hesitation. Alanna and Umar threw up walls of light, and Alanna summoned the apprentices again: "If you will do as the gods require you, come forth!"

The girls walked through the light together. Kara slowed, nearly stopping, for a moment, but both emerged. Alanna and Umar Komm created a deep trench in the ground before them. For the third time, Alanna summoned: "If you will do your duty by your people and your tribe, come forth!"

This task was the hardest, because it required the most determination. Few sorcerers lifted themselves from the ground; it cost too much strength to go a very short distance. Alanna doubted that she could do it, drained as she was by keeping Ali Mukhtab alive.

Kourrem hesitated, fighting to strengthen her resolve. She was forbidden to use thread, or to move rocks to fill the trench. She had to fly over it.

Kara stepped forward, her lower lip gripped between her teeth. Very slowly she floated across. She was nearly on the other side when Kourrem flew to catch up. Both of them collapsed onto the ground, exhausted. They stirred only when Umar Komm lifted Kourrem as Alanna lifted Kara.

"You are now shamans of the Bazhir," Alanna told her apprentices.

"Welcome to our Brotherhood." Umar Komm smiled.

seven

❧

The Voice of the Tribes

The next morning Alanna turned her duties over to Kara and Kourrem. "This way," she explained, "everyone knows you work with my approval and help. Have you decided which of you will be head shaman? If you disagree on something, one of you must have the power to make the final decision."

For a moment they looked at each other warily. Alanna knew she had given them a difficult choice, but she also knew *they* had to be the ones to make it, not she.

"Kourrem," Kara said. "She doesn't have trouble deciding things, the way I do. And she can stand up to the men better than I can."

Alanna hugged the taller girl around the shoulders. "If it was necessary, you could stand up to the men, Kara." She looked at Kourrem. "Do you think she is right?"

Kourrem shrugged, smiling ironically. "I don't know if she's right or not, but I'll be head shaman, I guess. We can't do everything without each other to help, in any case."

Alanna picked up her healer's bag. "I'll tell

Halef Seif and Ali Mukhtab," she announced. "For now, I suggest you continue your studies with the other shamans."

For the next fifteen days Alanna spent most of her time with Ali Mukhtab. The Voice was clearly failing; his flesh hung from his bones; his skin was gray, his eyes dull. Somehow he found the strength to teach Jonathan, his voice droning for hours as he fought to instruct the Prince in the many laws of the Bazhir.

During that time Jonathan worked harder than Alanna had ever seen him work before, both to master his studies and to win over the Bazhir headmen and lawmakers. Carefully and determinedly he sought out and spoke with each man, drawing opinions from them with a diplomacy Alanna did not know he possessed. It was at such moments that Jonathan seemed most alive and happy. The rest of the time he was restless and edgy, complaining about the sand and the heat and the lessons with Ali Mukhtab when he was alone with Alanna. He didn't ask her if she had made a decision about their marriage, and she was glad he hadn't.

Only once did he publicly lose his composure. Leaving the Voice's tent after her morning spellworking, she found the Prince waiting for her. He was frowning in a way she knew too well, lately.

"Let's go riding," he said abruptly, not appearing to see how worn and gray-faced she was. "I want to get away from here."

She stared at him. "Jon, we can't. He's ready for your lessons now."

"I don't care," the Prince snapped. "I've had lessons since I set foot in this village. I'm going riding." He turned away, and she seized his arm.

"You can discuss your boredom and whatever in private all you please," she hissed. "But the man in there is hanging on to life because *you* need to know what he has to teach you. I'd appreciate it if you stopped acting like a spoiled brat. If you want the Voice's power, you have to learn the Voice's lessons!"

"I didn't *ask* him to choose me!" Jonathan whispered hotly, putting his broad shoulders between them and the staring tribesmen. The Bazhir were startled to see them arguing, even if they couldn't be heard.

"But you're willing to take what he's offering!" she whispered back. "You of all people know everything has its price. And don't tell me you're tired of paying! This isn't the time, or the place!" She stared at him, until he looked away. Without another word he entered Mukhtab's tent.

That night he was all tenderness and apologies, and Alanna's anger faded. She loved him with all her heart. But marriage?

The next evening she and Myles dined alone in the tent she had been given after turning the large one over to Kara and Kourrem. Once the meal was over, she steeled herself to ask for her foster-father's advice.

"Myles, what happens when Jon marries?"

The knight glanced at her sharply. "The first duty of any noble wife is to give her husband an heir. The succession must be assured, particularly when a throne is involved; that is especially true for any woman who marries Jonathan. Should something happen to the King, gods forbid it, *and* to Jon, there are no close Conté relatives. Roger would have inherited had he lived—I know, that's what he planned!—but there was no one to succeed Roger. His father died when he was a boy; his mother died giving him birth."

"Like mine," whispered Alanna.

Myles nodded. "Sadly, it often happens. Roger's sole close relative was the King. The Contés rarely have large families," he added with a sigh. "Now there are only third and fourth cousins. It means civil war if Jon dies without an heir."

Alanna had nothing to say to this: Myles had confirmed her fears. She fought down panic, thinking, *I'm not ready to have children!*

"What?" Myles had spoken again.

"I said, did you accept Jonathan?"

"I still need to think about it."

"You do?" The man was obviously surprised. "The way he's been acting, I thought you said yes."

"Are you serious?"

"I see you together often enough. If he weren't sure of you, I should think he'd spend more time wooing you, winning you over. Well, perhaps I'm wrong. I'm not omnipotent." Myles picked up

Faithful and deposited the cat on his lap, stroking the animal's ears with gentle fingers. "Why are you still considering, if I may ask?"

"You remember what I said, about maybe Jon wanting to marry me for all the wrong reasons?" Myles nodded. "Well, nothing that's happened since has changed my mind. I know he's working hard, learning to be the Voice and getting the men of the Bazhir to like him, but when he's not dealing with them, he seems—well, spoiled. I never really thought he was that way at the palace. Any Prince is somewhat spoiled, of course. Wouldn't you be, with people buttering you up all the time?"

"I don't think either of us runs that risk," Myles said gravely, his eyes dancing.

"Perhaps responsibility would steady Jon," Alanna admitted with a sigh. "I don't think he's a bad person at all; in fact, I think he's a very good one. But lately I'm not sure if I like him very much. I keep telling myself he'll get over it, but what if he doesn't?"

"Many young women would give all they possessed to have your opportunity." There was no way now to tell what Myles was thinking.

"Not me," Alanna snapped, fingering the ember-stone. "I've been happy since I came here, and I like it. I don't want to give that up. I don't want to be well behaved, as a nobleman's wife should be. The King and Queen would try to make me stop dressing comfortably. They might even try to make me stop healing. I couldn't go wherever I wanted. No risks, and no adventures." She blushed with shame. "I love Jon, but I've got too many questions to decide to be hurried. I'm not certain I'm ready to marry, even if he is."

She was astounded to realize the look in her foster-father's eyes was of pride. "Few people are wise enough to know they might not be ready for such a venture. Too many rush to wed, only to discover they know little about what they're getting into. I'm pleased to see you put so much thought into this. By the way—I saw George Cooper before I left Corus."

"How was he?" Alanna wondered why Myles had brought up the King of the Thieves.

"He asked me to tell you he's moving to Port Caynn for a while. It seems the rogues there have been giving him trouble, so he plans to bring them into line." Myles drew a crumpled piece of paper from a hidden pocket; it had the address "House Azik, Dog Lane" written on it in George's scrawl. "He hopes you will visit him, if you can be released from your duties here."

❦

*A*lanna folded the paper, her heart leaping. To see George again! The she remembered Jonathan. As the Prince's bride-to-be, she might never be able to see George alone.

"I doubt if I can visit him," she announced, getting up. "Excuse me, Myles. I'm taking Moonlight for a run."

She hurried to the corral and saddled the mare, ignoring her common sense. Although the hillmen had not ventured near Bloody Hawk territory since Ishak's last battle, they might well be awaiting the chance to pick off a lone rider; it would be wiser to take a companion.

She headed for the open desert alone, wishing there was a way to ride so hard and fast that she left puzzles and heartache behind.

To be free—really *free,* she thought grimly as she brought Moonlight to a gallop. *To never worry about anything or anybody, to go where I want without thinking about other people at all....I've been carrying Roger and everyone else in Corus with me, just as I've carried the tribe since I killed Akhnan Ibn Nazzir. I wish the only one I ever carried with me was me—*

Hoofbeats sounded behind her; she wheeled Moonlight, bringing the crystal blade from its sheath in a swift movement. Then she smiled ruefully as she recognized Coram and his bay gelding.

I daresay I wouldn't be happy if I had no one but myself, she thought with a sigh, waiting for him to catch up.

ᔰ

*A*lanna began to sleep in Ali Mukhtab's tent, always ready with her Gift and medicines to bolster the Voice's fading strength. On the last day, when the moon would be dark, Mukhtab sent Jonathan to rest and to gather his resources. The lessons were complete; all that remained was the Rite itself. After shooing everyone out, Alanna placed the Voice in the deepest of slumbers, hoping to give him added strength for the night's ordeal.

Outside, she could feel a hushed tension in the village. To the tribesmen the selection of a Voice was more important than the coronation of a king. The Voice of the Tribes was priest, father, and judge to the Bazhir. Halef Seif had told her a Voice never acted without the approval of most of his people; the knowledge of Bazhir minds and hearts was far too heavy a burden for him even to consider defiance. This information convinced Alanna all the more that she never wanted to join with the Voice during those moments at twilight. She had trouble enough understanding herself; she wanted no one else—not even one supposedly as disinterested as the Voice—to know her thoughts and problems.

While the tribe ate the evening meal (there was no ceremony at the fire), Alanna went to Jonathan. The Prince had been fasting; now, dressed in a white burnoose, he looked pale and resolute.

"I wanted to wish you luck," she explained. She wasn't sure how to speak to him: he was preparing to take on a burden she would refuse at any cost. For a moment he looked as if he didn't know her. Then he stood, holding out his arms.

"Tell me you love me," he said, trying to smile. "I need the encouragement."

She ran into his arms, hugging him as fiercely as he did her. "Of course I love you," she whispered. "That part of it is settled."

He said nothing, continuing to hold her so tightly her ribs ached. At last she ventured, "Jon? Why d'you want to be the Voice? You're already restless."

"I *need* to be the Voice," he replied softly. "If I can do this thing, become the leader of the Bazhir, there should be few secrets of the human soul I won't understand. The Bazhir aren't so different from us, Alanna. If I know them, how they think, I'll know how most people think. With that knowledge I can become the greatest—the *best*—ruler who ever lived."

"It's so important to you?"

"It's what I was born to do," he told her, his voice harsh. "It's what I *will* do. In spite of being restless. In spite of everything."

∽

Jonathan and Ali Mukhtab stood at the summit of the hill with a fire between them, its flames reaching waist-high. Somehow the Voice stood alone—there was no one to catch him if he fell. Alanna waited with the other shamans some distance away: they were not permitted near until the ceremony was over; they were forbidden to use their magic.

Faithful stood on his hind feet, bracing his front paws on Alanna's thigh. Not taking her eyes off the scene before her, she picked him up, trying not to grip him too tightly. She was trembling with fear, because she had no control over what would happen.

Ali Mukhtab raised his hands, his voice suddenly strong as he chanted. The language was ancient, left from the time when the Bazhir lived in stone buildings on the other side of the Inland Sea; Alanna couldn't understand the words. She could, however, feel the power that began to fill the air: a dark, boiling force that drew answering chords from the crystal sword at her waist. She touched the hilt absently, mentally commanding it to quiet. The sound from the blade lessened, although she still could feel it quivering.

Ali Mukhtab ended his chant as suddenly-strong winds flicked burnooses across their owners' faces, raising little dust devils from the ground.

"Jonathan of Conté." Mukhtab's voice was soft, yet it rolled and echoed through the air. "You come, a northern stranger, seeking to be one with the Bazhir. For what reason should we permit you, son of the Tortallan King, to enter this most holy circle of our people?"

From the look on Jonathan's face, Alanna knew this wasn't part of the ritual. The Prince had to answer honestly, while the Bloody Hawk and the visitors from the other tribes listened.

Let it be the right answer, Alanna pleaded the Great Goddess silently.

A sudden burst of light turned the entire scene a blue-white color, dazzling them all. From the circle of light that blotted their vision, the listeners heard Jonathan's voice. "Because I know and honor your history, and I know and honor your laws. Because I never wish to see the Bazhir hunted and slain by our warriors, even as I never wish to see our warriors hunted and slain by the Bazhir." A soft chuckle swept through the watchers farther down the hills from the shamans, and Alanna felt a small knot of tension loosen inside her. Her eyes were beginning to clear, revealing at least the outlines of the two men above her. Jonathan continued, "Because only together will your people and mine become great. Because—" his voice grew very quiet. "Because I want to know the *why* of men and women."

ᖇ

There was a silence; Alanna was sure the thudding of her heart was audible to everyone. Then Ali Mukhtab raised his hands once more, his belt dagger glinting in his left fist.

"As the gods will, so mote it be!" he cried. A thunderclap made the ground rock beneath them as the Voice of the Tribes laid open a long gash in his right forearm. It was far longer than the ones Alanna had received when she became a Bazhir and when Myles adopted her. *Merciful Mother!* Alanna thought in horror. *He can't lose so much blood!*

Jonathan was opening a similar wound in his own right arm, paralleling the one he'd received on initiation into the Bazhir. Faithful jumped from Alanna's hold and raced up the hill to the two men. Alanna started to call him back, but Kara clapped a hand over her mouth, and Kourrem shook her head warningly. Alanna gritted her teeth, willing herself to stay where she was as Kara removed her hand. If either man saw the cat sitting now beside Mukhtab, he gave no sign of it. Their eyes were locked on each other's faces as the Voice stretched his bleeding arm across the fire to the Prince. Jon reached out and clasped the offered arm, both men drawing perilously close to the flames. The fire hissed as their combined blood dropped onto the hot coals.

"Two as One." Ali Mukhtab's voice was a broken rasp that rang in Alanna's ears. The power in the air climbed; Kara and Kourrem clung shivering to each other. Umar Komm reached over and gripped Alanna's shoulder. She covered the old shaman's hand with hers, grateful for the contact.

"Two as One." Jonathan sounded soft and halting, almost as if he were in a trance.

"Two as One, and Many." Ali Mukhtab's voice held a whining note that made the hair on the back of Alanna's neck stand straight up.

"Two as One, and Many." Jonathan shivered

uncontrollably. The fire suddenly roared higher than both men's heads, engulfing them in flames that were rapidly turning an eye-hurting white. Their burnooses began to smolder. As if he sensed her urge to run to them, Umar Komm tightened his grip on Alanna. He had warned her before the ceremony that she must not speak or interfere, no matter what happened. The gods would protect Jonathan and Ali Mukhtab, if they were meant to succeed.

"One—as—Many!" Ali Mukhtab forced the cry out as the blue-white flames caused many watchers to look away. The words thundered with magic, making Alanna's bones hurt and the crystal sword shiver.

"One!" Jonathan's voice was thick with pain, but he forced the words out. "As—Many!"

There was a crash of sound that left them deafened. For a moment Alanna thought she heard thousands of voices cry out in exaltation. Suddenly the fire went out; the darkness was split by Jonathan's scream. Alanna heard one—or both—of them fall. Umar Komm held her now with both hands, and a tiny part of her was surprised at the old man's strength.

At last everything was silent. The winds stopped and were replaced by a desert breeze. Umar Komm relaxed his grip on Alanna as the feeling of power oozed from the air.

"Now we shall see," he announced, bending to

pick up the staff he had dropped in order to hold on to her.

"Come," he ordered the shamans. They made their way to the summit of the hill. Others went to Ali Mukhtab as Alanna knelt beside Jon, feeling for his pulse with shaking fingers. His heartbeat was slow and strong. She seized his arm, preparing to tear a bandage from her robe—and stopped. Two scars, one reddish, the other blue-tinted, ran from the Prince's elbow to his wrist. The blue scar was warm to the touch, far warmer than Jon's body heat would have made it. She shivered. Ali Mukhtab had just such a scar on his right arm.

She looked up at Umar Komm. "He's all right." Glancing at the other shamans, who were lifting Ali Mukhtab, she whispered, "The Voice?" She knew the truth even as she asked.

Jonathan stirred and sat up, rubbing the blue scar. "I am the Voice of the Tribes," he rasped. "Ali Mukhtab, who was the Voice, has passed on. I remain." He stood, leaning on Alanna's shoulder, and the watchers below cheered until their throats hurt. Men came forward and took Mukhtab's body as Alanna rubbed away the tears flooding down her cheeks.

"He isn't gone," Jonathan told her. "He's here, inside me. They're all here—all the Voices." He looked up at a nearby man. "It won't be so bad, Amman Kemail. I am not wise, but I can always learn."

The big headman smiled thinly. "In your moment of becoming, we were each with you—" His eyes flicked to Alanna. "All save the Woman Who Rides Like a Man. You will do, Jonathan of Conté."

They gripped each other's arms. "If I succeed, I will owe it to the Bazhir and not to myself," Jon replied.

Halef Seif approached, bowing deeply to the Prince who had become their Voice. "It is time for our people to rejoice in a seemly fashion," the Bloody Hawk headman remarked. "Ali Mukhtab is delivered from his pain, and the Voice of the Tribes continues. Let us burn his abandoned shell, and send him to the gods with love. Come down to the village. We will remember Ali Mukhtab, and we will drink to our hope for peace."

∾

"What was it like?" Alanna asked Jon. They were curled up together, Faithful lodged between them on top of the blankets. Dawn was slipping sunlight through the tent flap.

For a long time he was silent. "It was the worst thing that ever happened to me," he said at last. "Even worse than the place between life and death, when you saved me from the Sweating Sickness. Worse than fighting the Ysandir, in the Black City. It was as if—" He drew a deep breath. "As if thousands of people were screaming inside my head, each wanting to be heard first. As if I were all of those people, only everything bad in our lives hurt more, because the feeling was multiplied. I lived all the lives of all the Voices; there have been four hundred and fifteen of us, Alanna. And I saw my own death. I was a chain. All my links were pulling apart. I lost Jonathan for a while; I was everyone *but* Jonathan."

"No wonder you screamed," she whispered, holding him as close as the cat between them would permit.

"But the things I could *see*." He had forgotten her now, remembering. "I could see the magic Faithful gave Ali Mukhtab to keep him alive. I could see the palaces we once had, on the other side of the Inland Sea. I could see us fleeing the Ysandir, and building Persopolis. I could feel the wind in our faces as we rode the sands, free from all kings. I could see the gods as they watch us live our lives. The Mother is beautiful," he said, his sapphire eyes shining with awe. "The most perfect woman, and not a woman at all. Mithros was so bright, the Black God without brightness, yet radiating peace. I could never do it again. But I will never forget that I'm One, and Many. When my life becomes too confining, when I feel I have no freedom, I can look into myself, and be someone else. I can *go* somewhere else." He turned and kissed her deeply, then added, "Alanna, for the first time since I was named, I am free."

～

When she left Jonathan's tent the next morning, Alanna found Halef Seif seated on the edge of the tribe's well, as if waiting for someone. He rose and walked with her as she went to the corral, watching as she got out combs and began to curry Moonlight. Finally he spoke. "The Voice of the Tribes must return to his home soon."

Bending down to reach her mare's hocks, Alanna grunted, "He was lucky to be able to get away this long."

"It will be good to have a Voice who is the son of the Northern King, even as it is good to have a shaman who is the Woman Who Rides Like a Man."

Alanna glared at the headman from under Moonlight's neck. "You haven't been so formal with me since I first joined the tribe," she accused. "What's on your mind, Halef Seif?" When he hesitated, she added, "I thought you, of all people, would be honest with me."

"Will you leave the tribe now?" he asked. "Will you be returning with him, to live in his house and be his wife?"

Alanna swallowed hard; this was being honest with a vengeance! "I don't know," she admitted, busying herself with the mare's tail. "I've been thinking about it, but I haven't come to a decision."

"He ordered his horses for today," the headman said implacably. "Surely he expects you to accompany him, if you will be his bride." Seeing Alanna turn pale, he added, "He ordered that your horse be prepared, too."

Alanna felt the beginnings of irritation. "He had no right to do that. I haven't given him my answer yet."

"Perhaps he believes he knows what your answer will be."

Alanna put her combs away. "I'd better talk to him." She slipped beneath the rope that enclosed the horses, and glanced up at Halef Seif. "No one is to ready Moonlight for a journey until *I* say so." She strode off, telling herself that Jonathan was tired, and had probably forgotten to ask her if she planned to go with him when he left today. For that matter, she remembered, he hadn't even mentioned he was leaving.

Relax, her sensible self remarked as she entered the Prince's tent. *Becoming the Voice would probably drive less important matters from his head—and he dare not stay here much longer.*

Jonathan was conferring with Myles and Coram. Already a boy from the tribe was packing his things. The Prince smiled at her. "My love, I've instructed Kara and Kourrem to pack for you," he announced. "If we leave after twilight, we should have several hours of cool riding—"

"May I speak with you alone, Jonathan? I know Coram and Myles will excuse us."

Seeing the scowl on her face, Coram needed no

further urging. He left. Myles looked from Alanna to Jon, plainly worried. "It's all right, Myles," the Prince assured him. "We'll be ready in an hour or so."

Myles stopped beside Alanna. "Don't say anything you might regret," he cautioned.

"I won't." Alanna gripped the ember-stone at her throat, telling herself that what she had just heard was rooted in a simple misunderstanding, one that would be made right. Myles sighed and walked out, closing the tent flap behind him.

"You didn't mention you were planning to leave today." In making an effort to keep her temper, Alanna sounded clipped and terse.

"I thought you knew." Jonathan was rolling up a map, not looking at her. "If I had been with anyone but Myles, my parents would have torn up the countryside looking for me by now. I must get back."

"I did not say I was returning with you, and you didn't ask me before you ordered people to do my packing."

"I assumed we'd begin preparations for the wedding. I didn't think you would want to wait."

"I haven't told you yes," Alanna reminded him, her voice tense.

He looked at her, startled. "But—I know how you feel about me."

"Being married to you is a great responsibility. I need more time to think about it."

"More time!" *He's actually amused*, Alanna thought, her anger mounting. "Be serious. After all these years, I'd think your answer is plain."

She had clenched her jaw so tightly it hurt to open it. "Not to me."

Jonathan slapped the rolled-up parchment onto the table, his patience nearing an end. "Stop it, Alanna. I've made enough allowance for maidenly shyness from you—"

"*Maidenly shyness!*" she yelled. "Since *when* have I shown maidenly shyness!"

"Keep your voice down!" he snapped. "Do you want the whole tribe to hear? What's gotten into you, anyway? I thought it was all settled."

"I said I wanted time to think!" Although her voice was quieter, her snapping violet eyes revealed her undiminished fury.

Jonathan's smile was full of masculine superiority. "That's what all women say when a man proposes."

"Do they indeed?" Alanna snapped. "And you're such an expert on marriage proposals, I suppose!"

"As much as you are," he snapped back.

"When I say I want time to think, I want time to think!"

Jonathan sighed wearily. "All right, you've had time to think. What's your answer?"

"That I need *more* time to think!"

Jon stared at her for a moment, color mounting

into his cheeks. "This is ridiculous!" he cried. "All right, I should've remembered you don't like people making plans without your say-so, but I thought everything was settled—"

"It isn't! How *dare* you take my acceptance for granted?"

"Well, *you* certainly didn't give me a reason to believe you'd refuse, did you?" he demanded, his hands clenched with anger. "Think carefully before you annoy me further, Alanna of Trebond! There are women who would do anything to marry me—"

"Then why didn't you ask one of them?" Alanna said. "You know what your problem is, Jonathan? You've been spoiled by all those fine Court ladies. It never entered your mind that I might say no!"

"And who would you take instead of me, O Woman Who Rides Like a Man?" he demanded. "I suppose George Cooper's more to your taste—"

"George!" she gasped, surprised at his new angle of attack.

"Do you think I'm blind? I've seen the way he looks at you!"

"What about all those women at the palace and the way they look at *you?*" Alanna demanded. "And I *know* you've had affairs with some of them! They've made you into a conceited—"

"At least they're *women*, Lady Alanna!" he said. "And they know how to *act* like women!"

Silence stretched between them, as Alanna

fought to keep from either slapping him or from bursting into tears. Finally she hissed, "I *refuse* to marry you."

Jonathan was now white with rage. "And I think I'm well out of a potential disaster!"

"Obviously!" she retorted. "Find yourself someone more feminine, Jonathan of Conté!" She hurled herself out of the tent.

Kara and Kourrem looked up from their packing, startled, as she marched into her own home. "I'm not leaving!" she snapped. "Next time someone tells you I am, check with me first!"

They bowed and hurried from the tent, their eyes wide above their face veils. Alanna threw herself onto her sleeping mat and gave way to furious tears.

Tears led to a long, exhausted sleep. When she awoke, it was dark. Jonathan and Myles were gone.

❧

"*J*onathan." Queen Lianne beckoned to her son. Jonathan obeyed the summons, trying to erase the frown that had creased his forehead since his return from the desert over a week ago. He could hear courtiers whispering now about his unusual surliness.

Let them talk, he thought savagely as he bowed before his mother's throne. *What do I care?*

His mother gestured for a willowy blonde to come forward. "Prince Jonathan," the Queen said as the blonde sank into a deep curtsy, "may I make Princess Josiane known to you? Josiane is the second daughter of the King of the Copper Isles; she has come to stay with us for a time. Her mother and I were good friends as girls. Josiane, my son, Jonathan."

Josiane looked up at him from her curtsy, her blue eyes huge with admiration. "Prince Jonathan," she said, her voice soft and husky. "It is an honor to meet the man who fought so bravely in the Tusaine War."

Jonathan took Josiane's hand and raised her to her feet, lightly kissing her fingertips. "I was just a boy then, Princess," he reminded her. She said nothing, her full mouth curved in a smile. "Would you care to dance?"

"I would love to." She moved gracefully out onto the floor at his side as Jonathan noted with satisfaction that she was tall (the top of her head level with his eyes), slender, and milky-skinned. *She'll do*, he thought with grim satisfaction. *She'll help me prove to that—female in the south that I never want anything to do with her again!*

eight

∾

The King of the Thieves

House Azik, Dog Lane, in the city of Port Caynn, was one of many large residences set off from each other by high walls. It looked like a respectable merchant's home.

"That a Trebond should come to the point of associatin' with thieves—with the worst of them all—" Coram grumbled as she tugged the bellrope.

"The *thief* is my best friend," Alanna reminded him tartly. "And *he* doesn't take me for granted."

She had tried to concentrate on tribal affairs after her fight with Jon, but her attention wandered constantly. It had been Coram's decision to accompany her when she decided at last to visit George; Alanna could only wish that he had decided to keep his tongue between his teeth when he did so. Coram had never approved of her friendship with George.

A brown-eyed, brunet young man peered out of the porter's door and yelped. Swiftly unbarring the large gate, Marek Swiftknife, George's second-in-command and perennial rival, let them in. "Quickly!" he hissed. "Before you're recognized!"

Once inside the courtyard, Alanna and Coram dismounted. Marek rebarred the gate and gripped Alanna's hand, his sharply cut, handsome face alight with glee. "It's still a jolt, seein' you with your chest unbound," he explained, ignoring Coram's warning growl. "And it's good t'see you, what with his Majesty sulkin' about, makin' life miserable for us all." He showed them into the house as he asked, "Where'd you get your skin so tan?"

"We've been in the desert," Alanna explained as Marek showed them into the house. "We're Bazhir now."

Marek shook his head. "If it isn't one thing with you—"

"Guests?" A buxom redhead came out of the shadows at the back of the main hall. "Who's come at this early hour?" Seeing Alanna, she laughed. "Well met, youngling. My cousin's goin' to be glad t'see *you*."

A hard elbow met Alanna's ribs painfully. "Introduce me," Coram growled into his knight-mistress's ear.

Grinning, Alanna said, "Rispah, this is Coram Smythesson. Coram was my first teacher; now he's my companion. Rispah is George's cousin and Queen of the Ladies of the Rogue," she added impishly.

Coram bowed over Rispah's hand. "How can I think ill of th' Rogue when such lasses are part of it?"

Rispah smiled. "I'm glad a strong-lookin' soldier like you don't wish to think ill of us," she replied, her husky voice a purr.

Shocked, Alanna realized they were flirting. Even more surprising was her realization that Coram was a fine figure of a man, big belly and all. *He's not even very old,* she remembered. *He's only forty or so. Plenty of soldiers wait that long to marry, till the itch is out of their feet....*

Feeling Alanna and Faithful watching with interest, Coram let go of Rispah's hand, blushing slightly.

He likes your coming here better now, Faithful commented from his perch on Alanna's shoulder.

A door slammed upstairs, and a male voice yelled, "Rispah! I asked for charts of the Merchants' Guild-House t'be sent up with my breakfast—"

"You have visitors, cousin!" Rispah called, winking at Alanna. "Right noble guests, if I'm any judge!"

Alanna put Faithful down on the floor, feeling uncertain and strange. What if George wanted nothing to do with her?

The tall thief rushed down the stairs and grabbed her, swinging her around as he laughed. "And I've been thinkin' you forgot me," he said, placing her on her feet once more. "Just look at you! Tan and fit and wearin' the clothes of a Bazhir—"

Alanna looked up into his friendly hazel eyes and broke into tears.

Rispah took Coram's arm with a smile. "I'll

show you t' your rooms," she said. "We'll be certain you and Lady Alanna have all you need."

After a worried glance at Alanna, who was sobbing into George's shirt, Coram shook his head and followed Rispah. The King of the Thieves looked down at Faithful, who watched them with unblinking purple eyes from his seat on the floor. "You, too," he said, jerking a thumb in the direction Coram and Rispah had taken. "Scat."

She won't tell you anything, you know, Faithful remarked as he obeyed.

"Will you not?" George asked Alanna, who was trying to wipe her eyes on the sleeve of her burnoose. He produced a large handkerchief from his breeches pocket and held it to her small nose. "Blow," he ordered.

Alanna took the handkerchief from him and blew her nose, then wiped her streaming face. "How long have you been able to understand Faithful?" she asked, her voice still choked.

"I understand him only when he wishes me to. Now, what're you cryin' for?" When she shook her head, he probed further, "Did somethin' happen while you were in the desert?"

"Yes," she said reluctantly, "but it had nothing to do with the Bazhir. *They* treat me with respect."

George's eyes widened. "You had a fight with Jonathan."

"I don't want to talk about it."

"He hinted to me when he was ready t'leave for

the South that he was planning t'pop the question."
Hope grew in the man's face. "Are you tellin' me
you refused him?"

"I *really* don't want to talk about it." Her voice
was forlorn.

George crushed her in a second massive hug.
"And you shan't," he whispered. "Come. Take
breakfast with me, and tell me what the Bazhir
tribes are like."

Sniffing, Alanna stepped away when he released
her, and followed him upstairs. "I can't believe you
don't know all about them," she accused. "You've
got eyes and ears everywhere else. Besides, surely
Lightfingers and his friend gave you a full report."

George grinned as he ushered her into his private rooms. "Ah, don't be holdin' my natural fears
for your safety against me. Besides, the lads saw
nothin' worth reportin'."

"All right." Alanna sighed as he closed the door.
"What would you like to know?"

◡

*I*t was an unusual company that George had
assembled in House Azik. In addition to Rispah
and Marek, there were three other rogues from
Corus: two large and muscular brothers named
Orem and Shem, and one small, whippy man called
Ercole. Another man was also present, Joesh.
Alanna didn't know him. He was dark and hand-
some, slender, with wide shoulders and a walk that

indicated almost perfect balance to Alanna's trained eye. She had no idea why he was there; but the other men, as well as Rispah's big female companion Harra, were present to help George deal with insubordination in Port Caynn.

"I don't know why it is," George explained that night as they sat before the fire and talked, "but all of a sudden the lads here thought they could take more than their share, and hold back what was meant for the city and my people. When I gently reminded them of their obligation to me, they actually said they wished t'be free of my rule." He shook his head. "I came here fast enough and dealt with their ringleader and principals."

Alanna, knowing quite well that George collected the ears—and sometimes the rest—of those who disobeyed his orders, hid a grin under her hand. She had no sympathy with thieves in the ordinary way, and none at all from any who underestimated George. "If it's all cleared up, why are you still here?"

"I thought to see if I can ferret out more discontent," he replied. "I also wished to have these rogues see I exist, and how I work. Mayhap I'm too aloof from my folk in the other towns and cities of Tortall, stayin' as I do in the capital." He looked at her frankly. "I've little to keep me there now."

"Don't, George," she whispered, feeling uncomfortable.

"All right, I won't," he said amiably. Silence

stretched between them until Alanna broke it.

"Who is this man Joesh? Is he new? I don't remember him."

George grinned as he settled more comfortably into his deep chair. "Joesh? He's no rogue. He's the Falcon of Shang, and a friend of Rispah's. I trust him to keep his mouth shut, or he'd not be here."

Alanna sat up, startled. "Another Shang warrior?" Unlike Jon, she'd never gotten the chance to see one of the legendary fighters in action. Whenever one had made a brief visit to the palace, she had been absent or involved in duties. To actually test herself against a man trained to fight from childhood....

George saw the thoughtful gleam in her eyes and shook his head. "Nay, lass, you'll not be challengin' him under my roof. I've no wish to see you killed by accident. These Shang lads are far quicker than the best knight ever lived, and you'll have to trust my word for that. Besides, I intend that you rest from bein' a knight whilst you're here."

"I've done nothing *but* rest from being a knight since I was made one," Alanna remarked bitterly as she sank back into her chair. "I'm probably getting rusty."

"Not you, lass." George laughed. "Never you."

ᴄ～

*A*lanna was not to find out if she was as good as Joesh; when she arose in the morning, the Falcon had left. George gave her no explanation for the man's departure, but she knew he had probably requested that Joesh go. She felt a twinge of regret for the chance missed, but only a small one. Life in House Azik was restful, and thoughts of challenging strangers to contests of arms were alien. George and his people went out of their way to keep her and Coram entertained, treating Alanna with a care and consideration she had never known, either as a page or a squire, or as the Woman Who Rides Like a Man.

On one crisp fall day Rispah took her to the markets of Port Caynn, where Alanna purchased two dresses, feminine underclothing and shoes, and a pretty shawl, using some of the monies Sir Myles sent as her allowance. Jonathan's taunts about her lack of femininity had stung and stuck, and the look in George's eyes when she appeared in a soft lilac wool dress went far toward healing those wounds.

George, in particular, was attentive to her needs and whims, taking time to walk with her on the beach, spending long evenings in games of chess, or just talking. Before, they had lived their lives under the scrutiny of the inhabitants of palace and city; now it was strange to be alone together, with only the household to know they were in Port Caynn at all. And if George was wooing her again, as he had done in the past, he was going about it very carefully.

"If he *is* courting me, I wish he wouldn't be so subtle about it," she confided to Faithful one night, after the thief had shown her to her bedroom. "But maybe he isn't. Maybe *he* thinks I'm unfeminine, too." Without warning, a tear trickled down her cheek, and she sniffed.

You're feeling sorry for yourself, Faithful replied without sympathy. *You provoked Jonathan into saying the things he did. You know how proud he is. If you hadn't pushed him, he probably would never have even thought you were unfeminine.*

Beet-red with rage, Alanna hurled a pillow at her cat, missing him completely. "You're as bad as Coram!" she yelled, forgetting where she was. "If it's all my fault, why do either of you bother to stay with me? Why don't you go and give Jonathan the benefit of your advice. I'm sure he'd appreciate it much more than I do!" She seized the door handle, intending to slam out of the room, and halted. The door was open, and George leaned against the frame, his muscled arms crossed over his broad chest.

"It's not polite to eavesdrop," she snapped.

"I don't doubt that," he agreed, his voice soft. "On the other hand, if you'd yelled a wee bit louder, perhaps Jonathan himself could've heard he had two unexpected allies here in Port Caynn." Reaching out, he touched her cheek with a gentle hand. "Lass—will you not tell me what passed in the desert?"

Alanna pulled away from his touch, unwanted tears trickling down her cheeks, "I can't, George," she whispered. "Don't ask me to—please."

He sighed. "Very well, then." Turning, he walked away, his feet making no noise at all on the stone floor. Alanna closed the door and let the tears fall, crying herself to sleep.

She slept late the next morning, breaking the habits she had set as a page, and awaking not long before noon. Still tired and bleary-eyed, she padded downstairs. The sound of George's voice coming from his study turned her away from the kitchen: thinking to turn his eavesdropping trick back on him, she crept to a spot where she could hear everything.

"She's that beautiful," George was remarking thoughtfully.

"One of your tall and shapely blondes," Marek's voice replied with enthusiasm. "Queenly, with lips a man would think were on the Goddess herself."

"Ye're certain the Prince returns her regard?" The low rumble was Coram's, making Alanna start with surprise. Why was Coram sitting in on a conference between George and Marek?

"Why, man, he's with her every moment of the day, treatin' her like they was betrothed," was Marek's reply. Realizing what they must be talking about, Alanna put her hand to her suddenly painful throat. "And their Majesties seem to approve. When Princess Josiane's not with him, she's got her head together with the Queen, plannin' the weddin', doubtless."

"But he hasn't asked her yet," George pointed out.

"The betting went from even odds to her favor the day I returned here," Marek answered. "Stefan at the palace stables says she couldn't've laid siege to him better if he was a castle and she the General of all the King's armies. The minute he returned from that mysterious trip away he had, they was introduced; and he's not left Josiane's side since."

"We'll want to keep this from the lass," Coram said worriedly. "She's been half-crazy since their fight; I don't want to think of what she'd do if she heard this."

Alanna slipped away from the door, biting a trembling lip. So Jonathan had found a replacement for her, and fairly quickly. She ran out onto the terrace, staring at the sea below. While she had been moping and making her friends unhappy and considering an apology, *he* had been dancing and flirting with an unknown but beautiful princess. He had not been serious about marrying her after all, and she had been acting the fool.

"How much did you hear?" George stepped onto the terrace, his eyes serious.

Alanna flashed a falsely bright smile at him. "Hear? Was I supposed to have heard something?"

He put an arm around her shoulders. "Lass, I'm not blind or stupid. You overheard Coram an'

Marek an' me talkin' about Jon's latest conquest. I can tell when you're about, did you know that? It's the only glimpse the Sight gives me of you."

Alanna started, surprised out of her misery. "I forgot you had the Sight."

"When it comes to you or anyone else with the Gift, it's well-nigh useless, since those with the Gift are veiled from those with the Sight. In any case, it's not as strong with me as it is with my mother. Still, I can feel you near me, and so I know you were eavesdroppin'." When she said nothing, he went on, "Will you tell me *now* what passed between you and Jon in the desert?"

Alanna's shoulders drooped, and she let him steer her to a seat on the terrace wall. He sat beside her, hugging her shoulders as she said quietly, "We had a fight." Slowly, haltingly, she told him all the details, not sparing herself. "Perhaps I was being falsely proud," she admitted when she was done. "Perhaps it wouldn't have done me any harm to go along with him and not make a fuss about asking me first. I didn't like the things he was saying, but I didn't want to chase him away, either."

"You're askin' the wrong man." George's voice was oddly hoarse. For the first time since she had begun talking, Alanna looked up and met his eyes. The thief swung her around to face him, resting his large hands on her shoulders. "I'm glad he showed you that nobles are a proud, ungrateful lot, thinkin' of no one but themselves."

"I'm a noble," she whispered, unable to look away from his hungry eyes.

"No. You're my own sweet lass, and all the woman I could ever want." He kissed her, pulling her close. Alanna struggled for a second, surprised, then relaxed, enjoying the kiss and the feeling of being held tightly and protectively. George pulled away, watching her face closely. "There's plenty more fish in the sea than Prince Jonathan," he told her softly. "And this particular fish loves you with all his crooked heart."

Alanna snuggled close, lifting her face to his again. "I'm glad," she said honestly. "I need to be loved right now. Kiss me again, please."

"Oh, no," George said, drawing in a ragged breath. "If I kiss you again now, one thing will lead to another, and this isn't the proper place for that sort of carryin'-on."

"Then take me to a place that is," she suggested. When he hesitated, she added, "I know what I'm doing, George. And it's not just because Jon found someone else. This should've happened between us a long time ago."

He stood, clearing his throat, "Well, then." Suddenly he laughed. "Come with me, darlin' girl."

∾

If Coram noticed that she had moved her things into George's room, he either said nothing or voiced his opinions to Rispah alone. Certainly he seemed happy that Alanna had left her fury and her self-pity behind. Rispah gave Alanna a big, lusty wink the first time she caught the young knight leaving George's chambers, and the thieves made no remarks at all. The only change at House Azik was in moods: people whistled at their chores; Marek teased the maids, and Rispah and Coram acted like teenagers in love.

Only one thing marred those autumn weeks in the house on Dog Lane: a growing feeling of power, radiating from Corus. At first Alanna ignored it, thinking it to be part of her depression. The sensation persisted, until she mentioned it to George. He reminded her that the only one in Corus who could focus that kind of power was Thom, and she sent message after message to her twin. If Thom wasn't the cause of the magic, he would know who (or what) was; but the young sorcerer never answered her letters. When she tried to communicate with him through the fire burning in George's hearth, two days before All Hallow, she found only a gathering cloud she could not penetrate.

"What do you see?" George asked softly as she stared at purple flames.

Magic, Faithful answered when Alanna gave no sign of hearing George's query. *All around the city. And no way to get through to Thom, whether he's causing it or not.*

George looked at the cat—he couldn't become accustomed to those occasions when he could understand Faithful—and grimaced. "Any way to find out if it's for harm?"

"I don't *sense* evil in it." Alanna sounded as if she was thinking aloud. "And Thom wouldn't thank me for riding into the city and disrupting one of his experiments."

If that's what it is, Faithful commented.

Alanna stared at the flames for a while longer. Suddenly, shaking her head to clear it, she clapped her hands, ending the spell with the command, "So mote it be!"

"You'll wait?" George asked, his eyes kindly. Alanna nodded. He reached down and helped her to her feet. "Then you may as well be comfortable while you wait," he grinned as he swept her off her feet and dumped her into bed.

∽

*A*ll Hallow dawned bleak and stormy. The waves battered the cliffs below the house, and the winds blew away anything not already fastened down. Alanna arose to find George gone, summoned to the city on a matter of business. His note said he hoped to be back by nightfall, but if he was kept too late he would stay at the Dancing Dove in Corus, rather than risk the return trip after dark. She wasn't to wait up, and she wasn't to worry. If she was good, he would bring her a surprise—and *not* stolen, either! Alanna grinned at this last, recognizing the joke behind many gifts George had given her and Jon in the years they had known each other. For a second the thought of Jon made her grim; but she soon brightened. George obviously loved her, and she had responded to her friend's love like a flower opening in the sun. Never before had she been coddled and treated like something precious. Jon had always treated her as a comrade, except when they were making love. She usually liked the way the Prince handled her, but a small, treacherous part of her longed for the gentle courtesy he gave noble ladies. Now George gave her that courtesy, as well as treating her like a comrade, and she liked the mixture.

Toward noon exhaustion hit her like a sledge-hammer. She was barely able to make it to her bed before falling into a deep, dreamless sleep.

When she awoke, it was pitch-dark, and the wind howled outside the shuttered windows. She reached out and ordered the branch of candles beside her bed to light, something she had done without thinking since becoming a shaman for the Bazhir. There was no flame in answer to her command, and when she looked inside, searching for her Gift, she found just a trace of magic. Only then did she discover the ember-stone was flickering with increasing urgency, and that the crystal sword was humming in its sheath as it had not in weeks.

While she slept, something had come and leeched away her Gift.

Lighting candles with a spill from the banked

fire, she headed for the library. Some extensive books of magic were there, and she had promised herself a look at them. Now seemed like an excellent time.

There was no sign of Faithful as she padded through the quiet halls. Marek and the other men had gone with George. Rispah and Coram would probably be in Rispah's chambers; and Rispah's woman friend, Harra, retired early. The servants had gone home for the night. Alanna felt all alone, odd and detached. She knew she ought to care that someone had tapped her Gift, but she couldn't.

It was nearly midnight when she closed the last volume, rubbing her eyes tiredly. As she had suspected, the only one with the power and the closeness to Alanna needed for such a tapping was her twin. She should have been angry, but her emotions felt dead. And she was getting sleepy again.

Suddenly she heard—and didn't hear—a boom, a crash that made even her dull senses quiver with alarm. The crystal sword shrieked and fell silent. Somewhere Faithful let out an anguished howl. Seconds later the door burst open, and the cat hurled himself onto Alanna's chest. She soothed him, caressing his fur and holding his shivering body close. It was fully an hour before he relaxed enough to let go of her tunic and settle onto her lap.

It's over, whatever it was, he yowled as he yawned. *He did the spell he needed all that power for.*

Alanna took him back to her bedchamber. No one else was stirring, so she and Faithful were the only ones able to feel whatever had happened. "We might as well forget it," she advised the cat as she hung the crystal sword on its hook. "I doubt Thom will give us an explanation."

To her surprise, when George returned the next day he brought a note from the young sorcerer. Thom had written:

> *Dearest Alanna,*
> *Perhaps this letter should have come to you sooner, but it was only when your friend George demanded an explanation that I realized you might be affected by my recent work. On All Hallow I will be attempting some experiments—all very arcane and esoteric, with no meaning for anyone but a Master, I promise you. The work is quite delicate and requires plenty of power. To get it, I'll be tapping you, since you never use more than a small part of your Gift. I know you won't mind. If I've caused you any inconvenience or worry, please forgive me.*
>
>

Your loving brother
> *Thom.*
>

"Well, I mind!" George snapped when she told him. "I could feel the city shake when he did his precious 'experiments'! Doesn't your twin have any regard for us lesser folk?"

Alanna had sent a blistering letter to her brother that morning, telling him the same thing. Now she grinned and shook her head. "He learned to be secretive in the Mithran Cloisters," she said. "If he can't be bothered to consult me beforehand, he certainly won't care about other Gifted people. Let's just be thankful he's doing experiments, instead of being up to real harm."

Thom's reply to her angry letter arrived before the week was out and extended his deepest apologies to his sister. With her Gift restoring itself, Alanna decided to let that be the end of the whole affair. She doubted that Thom would ever borrow her magic again without her consent. Obviously there were no other ill effects of his All Hallow's experiments.

∾

When the first snows fell, early in December, Alanna greeted their coming with dismay. George laughed as she unpacked her heavy clothing and covered herself with layers of silk and wool. She shrugged off his teasing, having endured its like from her friends for years. Now more than ever she missed the desert, and infrequent letters from Halef Seif only made her longing sharper. Recognizing her mood, George went to great trouble to find things to amuse and divert her; but in the week after Mid-Winter Festival ended, she spent an entire day poring over maps in the library.

"You wouldn't be thinkin' of leavin'?" he asked as they sat down to their evening meal. Coram and Rispah, who had joined them, looked anxiously at Alanna.

The young knight reddened and shrugged. "You could always come with me."

George arched one eyebrow. "Me? In the desert?"

"I suppose not," Alanna admitted gloomily as the new maidservant poured soup into her bowl. "It's just so *cold* here. And I'm getting restless."

She was lifting her spoon to her mouth when a frantic, yowling Faithful leaped onto the table sending Alanna's soup dish flying. The ember-stone sent out a burst of white heat as George yanked her back. Coram shoved his own dish away as Rispah ran after the fleeing maid. She returned within seconds, hauling the terrified woman back in a grip that permitted no careless movement on her captive's part.

Alanna extended her hand, and a wave of purple fire washed over the plates on the table. She looked up at George, her eyes sick. "They've all been poisoned."

George looked at Rispah. The redhead's mouth was set in a grim line; the maid fought her hold uselessly. "I think we'll learn a bit more if the noble lady isn't by," she told her cousin.

"You'll need me," Coram told them. He glanced at Alanna. "Wait in the library."

❧

*A*lanna didn't argue as Rispah, Coram, and George marched the protesting maid out of the room. Instead she went to the kitchen and questioned the cook, who was preparing to go home for the night. From her she learned that the maid, who had worked for them only two weeks, had come from Corus. She was supposed to be living with an uncle, but the cook suspected she got additional money from a local inn, where she entertained male guests. Still, she had done her work well and quietly, and it was hard to get good help during winter in Port Caynn.

"One last question," Alanna said, "and then I'll get Marek or one of the others to take you home in the cart. Did she have a letter from the Rogue in Corus, saying she was safe to wait on George?"

The cook turned indignant at the very thought that she would permit someone in the house who hadn't been cleared. From the house's account books she took the grimy piece of paper the maid had brought with her. Confirming the woman as safe, it was signed "Claw."

Orem escorted the cook home while Alanna gave the whole thing serious thought. It seemed likely that George had been the poisoner's target; since the deaths of Duke Roger and Ibn Nazzir, she had no enemies inclined toward murder.

"Who's Claw?" she asked when a tired, sweating

George came to the library an hour later.

The thief grimaced as he poured himself a glass of brandy. "One of the new young men in the city. Ugly as a goat—missin' an eye, purple marks on his face where someone threw acid on him once. Why?"

Alanna gave him the note admitting the would-be poisoner to his house, watching the thief's mobile face as he read. "Did the maid talk?"

"Hm? Oh, her. No more than that a man gave her the poison, and the money." He put the note down, rubbing his face wearily. "She ended too fast."

"Magic?"

George shook his head, slumping into his big leather chair. "Not that I could See. She was wearin' a charm about her neck. When we took it off her, she—died." Digging in his tunic pocket, he produced a small round medal hanging on a chain. "Have a look."

Alanna touched it, instantly feeling the evil as the ember-stone flared hotly. She yanked her hand away. "Throw it in the fire!"

Startled, George obeyed. The charm sputtered and melted. "Why?"

"It's been treated with a kind of poison." Alanna soaked George's handkerchief in brandy and held the dripping cloth out to her friend. "Wipe your hands with this—quickly! Did Coram or Rispah touch it?"

He obeyed, wrinkling his nose at the brandy fumes. "No, only me."

"Take off your tunic, and throw it in the fire. It's not magic; it's a poison taken from the fire-flower vines that grow in the southern hills. Farda, the midwife for the Bloody Hawk, told me about it."

"How does it work?" George asked curiously.

"You have to have contact with it over a long period of time, unless you drink it or it enters through a cut in your skin, something like that. As long as you *maintain* contact, you're all right. But if you run out, or if someone takes your source away—"

"You die," he murmured thoughtfully, watching the fire destroy his tunic. "And if someone was givin' it to you in your food, or some such, you'd never know." Startled, he looked at her. "Has it been in *our* food?"

She shook her head. "The ember-stone would have warned me, or maybe even Faithful." She glanced down at the cat, who had curled up by the fire. He yawned and twitched his tail over his eyes, indicating he didn't want to be disturbed.

"Claw, then," George sighed as she poured him another glass of brandy. "With a herb-woman to help, perhaps."

"What will you do?"

He shrugged. "What's to do, lass? I'll have to return to Corus and see what this Claw's been about." He put his glass down and drew her close. "Come with me."

Startled, she pulled back. "To Corus? George, I can't!"

"You have to face Jonathan sometime," he pointed out shrewdly.

"Not now, I don't! George, why do you have to go rushing back there? Come south with me. Let the thieves find someone else to rule them."

George shook his head. "I can't leave them when my position's weak, Alanna. Lads with reputations to make will be huntin' for me all my days, tryin' to kill me. And how do I know this Claw will do right by my people? I have as much responsibility to them as King Roald does to his own, as you do to your folk at Trebond."

Alanna clenched her fists. "And I can't go back to Corus. If I stay with you, I'll be recognized sooner or later. The scandal would hurt Myles; now he's my foster-father. If I go to the palace, they'll be after me to dress like a lady and get married and forget I ever won my shield."

George sighed. "That's everything, isn't it? I won't turn my back on the Rogue, and you can't leave off your adventurin'." He took her hand. "Come to bed. If I'm to ride for Corus in the mornin', we've a lot of good-byes to say first."

∾

When Alanna went south, a week after George returned to the city, Coram went with her. "Rispah will wait for me," he growled when Alanna questioned him about it. "We made an arrangement. She understands that if I'm not with ye, ye'll no doubt try somethin' daft. Now let an old man alone, will ye?"

Alanna dropped her questioning, glad to have his company on the long ride back to the tents of the Bloody Hawk.

nine

At the Sign of the Dancing Dove

*I*t was almost dark when George, Marek, and Ercole arrived at the gates of the city of Corus. They just made it in time; the greater gate was closed and locked behind them for the night. Now travelers would either have to enter the city on foot, or turn back to a nearby wayhouse until the gates were opened at dawn. All three men were tired. The ride from Port Caynn, which normally took only half a day, had been filled with battling winter wind and sleet.

"We've had easier travels afore now, Majesty," Ercole remarked as they turned their horses into the long alley that led to the stables at the rear of the Inn of the Dancing Dove. "Warmer, too."

It was far darker in the alley than on the torchlit main streets, and George felt uneasy. Bringing up his chestnut mare, he scanned the shadows. Noticing their chief's wariness, Marek and Ercole began to search the dark, too, readying their long staffs. Only George dared carry a sword openly, as Tortallan commoners were not permitted them.

George let his mare inch forward until he spotted an overhang. Smiling grimly, he kicked the mare into a jump. The man on the overhang leaped a second too late, falling behind George. Other masked attackers surged out of connecting alleys and doorways; George ran one through and wheeled to catch a second as he grabbed for George's saddle. A quick glance told him Marek and Ercole remained horsed, in spite of attempts to unseat them.

George's mare reared and knocked the man trying to cut her saddle girths flying. The thief grinned—not even his most trusted people knew he had trained his favorite mount to fight like any noble's war-horse, as her Moonlight fought for Alanna. The mare he had named Beauty curvetted, her rolling eyes searching for someone else stupid enough to get in range of her hooves.

Marek yelled and clutched his shoulder, where a dark flower blossomed against his light-colored jacket. Distracted by his henchman, George didn't see the man on the roof overhead until he leaped onto George's back.

They grappled for the knife the other man held, George using every trick he knew to dislodge his enemy. The attacker was strong, stronger than George, but he had forgotten the thief-king's almost supernatural speed. Twisting into a position that made his back scream, George got one hand free. Flicking the knife he carried hidden in his sleeve into his hand, he stabbed his attacker in a rapid-fire movement. The man gasped and fell off, rolling into the snow.

As if his death was a signal, the others broke and ran. George would have pursued them, but Ercole reminded him that Marek was hurt. The younger man was slumped in his saddle; blood dripped freely down his arm into the slush on the ground.

Ercole wiped his knives on his sleeve and slid them back into sheaths at his wrist. "They didn't offer a sound, Majesty. Not a word."

"So we can't guess who they are, doubtless." George hoisted Marek up, wishing just once for Alanna's way with fire. "Will you make it to a safe place, lad?"

Marek grinned weakly. In the bits of light that came from the houses and shops on the alley, his handsome face was pale. "All these years I've tried to take your throne from you, George; now we both have to fight some—usurper!"

"Can you hold up a bit more?"

"Aye." Marek boosted himself erect in his saddle. "Lead on, Majesty."

George took the rein of Marek's horse and headed down a second alley, thinking hard. Until he knew the nature of the enemy, the Dancing Dove was not safe for him or the people closest to him. He led Marek and Ercole to the back of his mother's walled house, trusting that his enemies had not set a trap there as well. He was reassured by snow piled around the small barred gate; no one had walked here recently. Dismounting, he used his keys to undo the double locks before taking Marek and Ercole inside. The young man was slumped over, and Ercole held him in place with one hand.

"The stables are over there," George told him quietly as he slid Marek off his horse. "Unless we've other guests hid within, this place's safe."

"Get the lad inside," Ercole advised. "He's bleedin' heavy still."

A second pair of keys let George into his mother's kitchen. A kettle was on the hearth, but otherwise the room was dark. Carefully placing Marek on a bench by the big table, the King of the Thieves slid out into the rest of the house, his every sense on the alert. The ground floor was dark—*odd, for it's not even suppertime,* he thought. Then he stiffened against the wall, hiding himself in the shadows below the stairs leading to the second floor. A woman not his mother was descending.

In a swift movement he had the lady in his grip, one large hand over her mouth. "Don't scream," he advised. "Tell me what you're doin' in Mistress Cooper's house."

He took his hand away, and the woman drew a slow, shuddering breath. "She's ill. I'm a healing-woman, come to stay with her till she's better." She faced George, and indignation lit her brown eyes. "George Cooper, such a fright you gave me! What d'you mean, sneaking into your mother's house like a thief!"

Recognizing her, he grinned. "Mistress Kuri, I

am a thief." As she gasped with shock, he added, "What's wrong with my mother?"

"I don't know. Since All Hallow she's been as weak as a new kitten. Only now does she get her strength back."

George looked upstairs. "I'll go to her as soon as may be. Meanwhile, I've a patient of my own who needs lookin' after."

Kuri shook her head mournfully when he brought her to Marek. She got the wounded man braced on her shoulder easily, handling him as if he weighed nothing at all. "Open the door to the work chamber." George obeyed and lit the lamps as Kuri gently placed Marek on the long table. "I'll need boiling water. Make yourself useful," she commanded, cutting the jacket away from Marek's shoulder.

Back in the kitchen, George put the kettle on to boil as Ercole warmed his hands. Telling the older man the situation in the house, George placed him at Mistress Kuri's orders before running upstairs to his mother's bedchamber.

Eleni Cooper looked at her son, her hazel eyes alert. "I thought I felt you in the house. Did you frighten poor Kuri to death?"

"She seemed unshaken to me. What's happened? I saw you not long before All Hallow, and you were fit enough then."

"I tried probing someone's magic too deeply. The guards set on it were *very* strong."

"Thom!" George hissed. "By the Dark God, Mother, if he's hurt you with his precious 'experiments'—"

"Lady Alanna's brother? I should have guessed. Only *he* has such power, these days." The woman shook her head. "If only I knew what he was up to!" She sighed and returned her attention to George. "And what are you doing here, at this hour? I thought you'd be stuck fast to Lady Alanna's side."

He shook his head, looking away. "We've parted, Mother—she to go adventurin', and me—"

"This house has been watched for five weeks now." She read his thoughts, as she always had. "A man who wouldn't give his name tried to question the girl I have in to clean. She has her orders, though, and she won't talk against my wishes."

George could hear Mistress Kuri's uncompromising tread on the stairs. "I'll be goin' out again, as soon as I've made sure Marek is well."

"Young Marek is hurt?" She had never met him, but George had often entertained her with stories of Marek's attempts to get the throne of the Rogue for himself.

"He'll survive," Kuri announced, having heard her question from outside. "He lost a deal of blood, though, and I put him in one of the small restchambers."

"But he'll live?" Only now did George betray his anxiety for his long-time rival and sometime friend.

"He'll live, and cause more trouble, I don't doubt."

George nodded, relieved. "Mother, I need house-room for myself and another of my men, only for tonight. We'll go to earth elsewhere tomorrow."

"Of course." His mother's voice was serene, but her eyes were worried. "George—"

"I can't help bein' crooked, Mother," he said. "And this is the price I must pay." He kissed her cheek and looked at Mistress Kuri. "I'll be takin' Ercole with me. We'll let ourselves back in."

"I'm sure you will," the healer replied severely. George laughed and patted her cheek before seeking Ercole out downstairs.

They were outside the walls of the house with the doors locked behind them before Ercole asked, "Where might we be goin'?"

"The Dancin' Dove," George said grimly before pulling a wool muffler over his chin. Ercole swore fluently and followed him.

∽

As a noble studying to become a knight, Alanna had spent a good amount of time at the inn called The Dancing Dove. This was George's headquarters, the royal palace for the thieves who swore allegiance to the Rogue. It was the place they gathered when they were not about their business as thieves. There were a number of entrances and exits, some known only to George and Old Solom, the innkeeper. George and Ercole entered through one of these, emerging in the darkened hallway that stretched behind the stairs to the upper stories. Sheltered by the dark, they could watch the entire common room, filled to its rafters with thieves, prostitutes, flower sellers, fences, forgers, peddlers, fortune-tellers, healers and sorcerers with small Gifts, merchants doing secret business, rogue priests, even a nobleman or two. Old Solom and his maids bustled about, serving food and drink while keeping a watchful eye on the table beside the great hearth—the place where George was wont to sit.

George smiled grimly. Nearly all of the people in the common room were quiet and fearful. When *he* sat by the fire, the din was so loud a man couldn't hear himself think. Now the loudest noises were made by Solom or the maids.

The man named Claw was at George's table, although not, the thief-king noted, on George's "throne." His back was to the two men in the hallway, and only his immediate friends—three vicious brutes George would not want at *his* back—sat with him. George searched the room for his own court and found Scholar in a drunken huddle on the other side of the fire. Lightfingers was nowhere to be seen. Rispah was still in Port Caynn, but Orem and Shem were at the back of the room, playing dice.

Making sure each of the six knives he carried

was ready, George nodded to Ercole. Stepping into the light, the older man at his back, he tapped Claw on the shoulder. "Thanks for keepin' it warm for me, friend," he drawled in his sweetest voice.

Claw jumped, knocking over his tankard. Brown ale spilled unheeded over his breeches as he stared at George. "But—you—"

"I know, I said I'd be stayin' in Port Caynn a bit longer," George said agreeably. "But there! I got that lonesome for all these friendly faces, and that bored without you lot keepin' me on my toes." Orem and Shem had moved to the front door and were guarding it with drawn knives. Two other men George knew he could trust came to cover the rear exit and Ercole's back. "You're drippin'," he added, sliding onto his "throne." Not for a second did his eyes leave Claw. The man had a reputation for doing the totally unexpected, and he might be crazy enough to attack George now.

Claw stared at George for a long moment, his single pale eye unreadable. Finally he turned and snapped to his henchmen, "Why are you goggling at me? Get a cloth or something, and mop up this mess." His eye swiveled back to George's face. "Welcome back, Majesty." He ignored one man's clumsy efforts to wipe the ale from his breeches. "I trust your journey home was uneventful."

"A bit chilly." Claw had lost his initiative, but it still paid to take no chances. George accepted a tankard of mulled wine from Solom without looking at the old man. "Has all been quiet here?"

"Quiet as the Black God's temple." At last Claw moved away from the table, his men at his back.

"Don't go," George said, waving an expansive hand. "Sit with me and tell me what's passed, these weeks I've been away. 'Twould be a pity if I'd patched up my trouble in Port Caynn to find it fostered here."

The one-eyed thief hesitated, and George hoped that the man would be mad enough to refuse. It would be all the excuse he needed, and Claw could never hope to equal him with knives. Then Claw snapped at one of his men, "Get me a clean chair!"

The man hurried to obey as George realized, *Claw talks like a noble.*

"Let me buy you a drink." George smiled, beckoning Solom over. "I've a bone to pick with you, my friend."

Claw shook his head when Solom offered him wine, and with a shrug the innkeeper refilled George's tankard. "What could I have done to give offense, Majesty?" Claw asked, his face blank and innocent.

"You cleared a maidservant to wait on me and mine in Port Caynn, and she tried to poison me. Surely you looked into her background, Master Claw?"

"A maidservant? I sent no maidservant to wait on you," the other thief replied.

George slid the grimy slip of paper across the table for Claw's scrutiny. The one-eyed man looked it over carefully, turning it this way and that in the light as he pursed his lips. At last he shook his head and returned the paper. "It's a truly excellent forgery," he announced calmly. "But it is a forgery, nonetheless. I never wrote this letter."

"You're certain?" George asked quietly. "Best think hard, for I'd not appreciate hearin' otherwise at some future date."

"Ask anyone in this room," Claw offered, gesturing widely to their staring audience. "Did I ever send a serving woman to wait on his Majesty at the Port?"

Heads were shaken slowly as George realized (with some admiration) that Claw had found the perfect excuse. With no witnesses and the woman dead without having named her sponsor, he was in the clear.

"You're lucky, Friend Claw," he told the younger man. "Mayhap you'll always be so lucky: to be innocent of the plots of others, of course."

"I hope to be, Majesty," Claw replied with a tiny smile. "I do not wish to become involved in any losing propositions."

∽

When morning dawned, the common room had emptied of all but the people George knew to be loyal. He had learned nothing from Claw, although he had kept his rival at his side all night. That was to be expected. The learning would come now, from sources he trusted.

One by one he sent his people out on errands, to talk to other thieves, to find those who had not been present and to learn why, to learn who was Claw's and who was not. He sent them in pairs, warning them to watch their backs. Shem returned to Port Caynn with a note asking Rispah to return as soon as Alanna and Coram were on their way. George needed her when it came to dealing with the women who followed the Rogue. They obeyed him, for his looks and his charm, but Rispah knew their secrets.

Finally only Scholar was left. Even Solom had retired to his upstairs room, exhausted with the night and its anxieties.

"Be discreet, but find me Sir Myles of Olau," George told the old forger. "I'll need him here, disguised, by nightfall."

Scholar nodded and polished off the last of his mulled wine. "I know where he's to be found. And, Majesty—" George looked up, surprised to see tears in the old man's eyes. "It's glad I am you're back. That Claw's a bad 'un."

As the door closed behind Scholar, George permitted himself a heartfelt sigh. Ercole moved out of the shadows, looking as tired as his chief. "Do we sleep here?"

George shook his head. "I don't propose givin'

Claw my head on a platter. We return—discreetly—
to my mother's house."

"And tonight?"

"I've a better hideaway in mind for tonight."
Standing, he clapped Ercole on the shoulder. "Let's
go. I want to see how Marek's doin'."

⌣

Myles peered at Claw through the peephole in
the false wall of the common room. Behind him
George waited. Old Solom would draw Claw into
talk as they sat in front of that very spot, and Myles
would be able to hear every word.

After a second the knight drew back and nodded. Silently George led him away from the hidden
spot, taking him upstairs to the chambers where he
lived in more peaceable times. There he poured
Myles a brandy, waiting till the older man had
refreshed himself before asking, "Well?"

"No doubt about it," Alanna's foster-father
replied. "Claw was born noble and was well edu-
cated, for a time, at least." He frowned, shaking his
head. "The problem for me is that I _know_ his voice.
I've heard Claw speak before, and not as a thief,
either." He held his glass out for a refill. "Perhaps
my daughter is right: I should stop drinking."

George grinned. "Let me congratulate you, sir,
on adoptin' Alanna. 'Twas a kind-hearted thing to
do."

"It was kind of her to let me," Myles demurred.

"If only she could straighten things out with Jonathan; no offense to you, George, but I *do* miss having her at Court."

"As I miss havin' her here," the thief reassured him. "Speakin' of my lass—have you any idea what it was that precious brother of hers was up to, at All Hallow?" He told Myles what had happened to his mother.

The knight sighed and shook his head. "I know that a number of people in the palace with the Gift were angry with Thom for days afterward. I've been hearing some odd rumors—" He stopped for a moment, as if unsure of what to say, then went on. "I have reason to believe Thom may have been trying his hand at—raising the dead."

George didn't try to mask the horror in his eyes. "The dead! Is the lad insane? The dead are meant to stay so!"

"I overheard some conversations he had with Lady Delia," Myles went on. "She seemed to be taunting him, saying that if he were truly the most powerful wizard living, he could raise the dead, as Kerel the Sage was said to have done. A number of the younger people in the palace have been trying to ascertain the full extent of Thom's powers. I think they regard it as a game."

"A game?" George whispered. "A *game* of settin' the world by its ears, callin' on power no man should use for casual purposes?"

"That is what I believe," Myles agreed somberly.

"Perhaps I'm wrong, George. I tried to talk with him, but I think his pride was offended when I made his sister my heir. He taunted me with half-truths and stories, nothing definite, not even an outright lie. I know you have weighty matters on your mind, but—"

"What could be weightier than such as you believe?"

A smile crossed the knight's face; and for the first time George realized how frightened Myles must be. The smile took ten years off his age. "If you would approach Thom? Being that you are— who you are—"

"And as respectable as I am?" George suggested with a grin.

Myles grinned back. "As a matter of fact, yes; Thom may talk to you, or at least reveal more of the truth."

"And I have my own grievance to make with the lad," George reminded him, remembering his mother's worn face. "As soon as I get a hold on what passes here, I'll be up to the palace."

Myles rose, gathering up his cloak. "I'll start inquiries about Claw," he promised. "Injuries such as he has, particularly the acid scars, are difficult to come by. They are even more so when you're nobly born."

George gripped Myles's hand. "You're a good friend, Sir Myles. Be assured I won't forget."

After showing the knight out, George returned

to hold court once more at the Dancing Dove. Once again he stayed there all night, seeing who was there, being seen. Bits and snippets of information came to him over the next few days as Rispah and Shem returned and went to work. No further attempts on his life occurred, although word of a costly jewelry theft that had not been cleared with him reached his ears. After a week had passed since Rispah's return, he gathered all those close to him in a room hidden beneath the streets that formed the marketplace.

As they compared notes, the picture the thieves saw forming was a bleak one. "He's got nearly half our people, with bribes or fear," George summed up. "He must've been plannin' this a long time, before he came to the city, even. He's been workin' through the likes of Zorina the Witch and Nave the Fence, gettin' his hooks into us." He sighed. "We'll have to move slow, then. Buy our folk back, and destroy the secrets he's got against them."

"Why?" Marek wanted to know. "Why not just kill him and be done with it?"

"Because one of his people will come forward to take his place," George replied. "I want his entire organization, not just him. Because he's got help, and I want to know who it is. And I want to know who *he* is, why he's not challenged me like any other Rogue would've done."

"And if he wins?" Rispah wanted to know, her brown eyes worried.

"If he wins, then I don't deserve to be master here." George's face was grim. "If he wins, I've no guarantees he won't betray every one of us to my Lord Provost, or someone worse, because I don't know what he wants. Where he is placed now, he can rule us or destroy us. Do any of you care to wager which it is?" There was no answer; he really didn't expect one. "You all know what to do and where to ask your questions, then. As soon as the passes open eastward, I'll send someone to find out what he was in Galla before he came to us."

～

Thom, Lord of Trebond and the youngest living Mithran Initiate, poured a glass of wine for his guest, a mocking smile on his lips. "You can't imagine what a pleasure it is for me to have my sister's—friend—come to visit," he said. "Particularly when it may be as much as your head is worth to be seen here, in the palace."

"Why not call me Alanna's lover, and be honest about it?" George suggested. The purple and gold brocade robe Thom wore over his stark black shirt and hose hurt the eyes; its cost would have fed a poor commoner and his family for a year. "As it is, I have a number of things I care to discuss with you. I couldn't be waitin' for your next excursion into the city to meet you."

"Particularly since I never go to the city," Thom agreed. "So Alanna has returned to the desert, with the devoted Coram in tow. How selfless of her. Unless she was afraid Jonathan might convince her to take back her refusal? She needn't have worried; he's very much occupied with Princess Josiane these days."

George stared at Thom. *If my lass had made no friends, only enemies,* he thought, *and if she'd been too frightened to let others know she was a human bein', disguise and all, she might well have turned out like this monster. He's all brain and cynicism now, with no heart left to him.* "Well, you're a nasty bit of work, aren't you?" he remarked amiably. "Why don't we talk of your goin's-on here durin' All Hallow?"

A look of grudging respect entered Thom's violet eyes. "I'm sure I told Alanna *and* you I was working on experiments."

George made a disgusted face. "And *I'm* sure it was no such thing. Didn't you feel my mother testin' your guardin'-spells? Or were so many tryin' to learn what you were up to that you took no notice of those left half-dead?"

"I felt someone test the ward," Thom admitted. "But I was—busy. I'm sorry it was your mother who was harmed, but she had no business prying into that kind of magic. She's fortunate to be alive."

"Glad you think so. And what experiments are so important that you must put such spells to protect them?" When Thom didn't answer, George pressed, "Who were you tryin' to raise from the dead?"

Thom jumped to his feet, the mocking expression wiped from his face. "You dare to question me, George Cooper?" he yelled, fury radiating from him in waves. "Your relationship with my sister means nothing here, so do not think to try my patience!"

George stood, his hazel eyes grim. "Don't think to threaten me, laddy," he warned softly. "I won't stand for it."

"I have nothing more to say to you," Thom gritted. "Get out."

"I'll take my leave, then," George replied. "But I don't need my Sight to tell me you're in trouble, great sorcerer or no." He hesitated, then said wryly, "Doubtless I'll live to regret this, but for your sister's sake you may call on me in need."

Thom drew himself up. "I am more than able to handle my own affairs."

"Is that why you're shakin' so?" George inquired. "Best have a shot of brandy to steady your nerves, my lord. I'd hate to think there was anythin' in this world of ours could be beyond the skills of one such as yourself." Bowing mockingly, he left Thom.

And there's not a thing I can do or say, until I know what's ridin' him like the Old Hag of the Graveyards, the thief told himself grimly as he slipped out of the palace. *But I'll bet every knife I own he's gotten himself into trouble that won't easily be fixed.*

George smiled. Trouble with the Rogue, trouble with Thom. The future looked exciting. At least he wouldn't be bored. And as long as he kept his wits about him—it was good to be back in Corus.

ten

The Doomed Sorceress

*I*n a way it was disappointing for Alanna to find the Bloody Hawk had done very well for themselves in her absence. No problems had arisen that Kara and Kourrem could not handle with Umar Komm's advice. The school for sorcerers was learning the many forms of fire-magic, something Alanna had explored as far as she wanted to. She diverted the shamans for an afternoon to the problem of Lightning (which remained broken despite all the spells she tried), but their efforts to repair it came to nothing. The last try blew down several tents and brought Halef Seif to command them to stop while within the village precincts.

Discouraged, Alanna often went riding alone, deliberately returning after sunset to avoid the moment they joined with the Voice of the Tribes. She only missed Jon at those times. She missed George with a sullen ache that refused to go away, because of all people George made her laugh.

She was grooming Moonlight after one ride, wondering what she would do now, when Halef Seif found her.

"You are restless," he commented. "What troubles you?"

Putting her mare's combs away, she replied, "Did you know six days ago I celebrated my first year as a knight?"

"Coram mentioned it," the headman admitted.

"Anniversaries make me think. I've been remembering all that's happened since I won my shield." Falling into step together, they walked toward the hill overlooking the village.

"You slew the Sorcerer-Duke."

"You know, Halef Seif, I don't dream about that much anymore. Maybe it was a waste, and I acted too quickly, but it's over. So much has gone on since then. I came here, I met you and Kara and Kourrem—"

"Ishak also," he reminded her as they slowly climbed the hill.

Alanna nodded; her mouth twisted sadly. "I guess what happened to Ishak taught me I can't punish myself for things that are over and done. After all, I had to get on with teaching Kara and Kourrem, not with mourning him. And I'm proud of the girls."

"They are pupils to make any shaman proud. Any tribe, for that matter." At the hill's summit, he bowed, indicating a flat-topped rock was to be her seat. Alanna laughed and dusted it off, noticing the blackened spots around it from the magic she had worked here with her apprentices, and the scorch-marks left by Jonathan's Rite of the Voice. She sat, and Halef Seif knelt beside her, watching the village.

"You know, it's funny—I've learned more about other women since coming here than I ever did before. Pages and squires don't spend much time with women, and besides—" She grinned. "I was notoriously shy when it came to girls."

Halef chuckled. "And so you've discovered you like your own sex?"

"How can I not like other women?" Alanna inquired. "Particularly after knowing Kara and Kourrem and Mari Fahrar and Farda? I don't feel nearly as odd about being female as I did before I came here."

"But now you must be moving on?" he asked gently.

"I hate it when I'm not doing something useful," she admitted. "After spending all those years studying things or performing duties around the palace, I've gotten into the habit of working. With Kara and Kourrem doing so well, there's nothing for me to do. I've been thinking of riding south with Coram, to see what I can find."

"I know of a task for you, if you wish it." There was a note of diffidence in the headman's voice she had never heard before.

"Name it."

He smiled reluctantly. "I have a friend, a woman who is a sorceress in Alois, near Lake

Tirragen in the hill country. For three nights I have dreamed she was in peril, cut off from me by fire." He shook his head. "We grew up together, before she discovered her Gift. She could not stay. There was no Woman Who Rides Like a Man to say she could be a shaman. But she returns here often."

Is she the reason that Halef Seif never married? Alanna wondered.

"I would go to her myself, but my duties do not permit such freedom—"

Alanna put her hand on his arm. "I'll go. Don't worry about your friend. If she's in trouble, I'll do everything I can to help."

For a moment he covered her hand with his, the lines of concern smoothing out of his face. "Thank you, Alanna."

ᴗ

*A*lois was five days' ride to the north through hill country. Coram and Alanna donned leather and mail for the trip instead of burnooses; Alanna made sure her uncovered lioness shield was prominently displayed. Dressed as Bazhir, they might have encountered trouble. Dressed as Tortallan soldiers, they did not glimpse another soul.

During the ride Faithful stuck close to Alanna, never straying. The knight knew her pet was worried. "What's going to happen that you aren't telling me?" she finally demanded when they passed the marker indicating the village was near.

I don't know, Faithful admitted. *I just have a bad feeling.* He settled down in his cup, the tip of his tail switching anxiously.

It was a beautiful day for January. The breezes were warm, and the snow had melted from the ground. Alanna expected children to be playing outside the huts that grew thicker as they approached the village, but no one was in sight. If people watched from inside their homes, there was no sign. A noise disturbed her, and she jerked around in her saddle. Coram was taking the canvas wrapping from his round leather shield, his dark face grim.

"I don't like what I'm feelin' here," he admitted. "Do ye?"

Alanna grimaced and undid the fastenings that held her shield over Moonlight's haunches. Settling the lioness rampant on her left arm, she drew the crystal sword with her right. *It doesn't even hum at me anymore.* Then she heard people shouting in anger and fear. It was impossible to make out the words, but the voices came from the village's center, behind the first wall of huts.

They trotted forward, scanning watchfully now as they made for the source of the cries. No one ran out to greet them; the huts of the village proper were as deserted as those outside.

There was a mob in the wide space that was the heart of the village: a tall, angular man in tattered gray robes stood on a platform that raised him head and shoulders above those around him. Alanna's senses prickled with uncomfortable recognition before she and Coram stopped beneath the eaves of a large cottage. They examined the area for armed men (other than the villagers, who waved sticks and farming tools), waiting to see what the fuss was about.

"Yahzed will have your souls," howled the man on the platform. His wide eyes gleamed with fanatic joy. Behind him a tall post thrust against the sky; the sight of it made Alanna sweat. Where had she seen this picture before? "Yahzed is angry; he is ferocious! Obey his command! Cleanse yourself of the ancient evil or Yahzed comes with plague and famine to cleanse *you!* Obey the servant of Yahzed! Only then will you escape the wrath of the God of Stones!"

A knot of men, struggling with something, encircled the tall post. Alanna remembered: twice she had seen this place, and the madman exhorting the people. Only in her second vision, the one given to her when Ishak had destroyed himself, she had seen a woman burning at the post.

A knot of villagers struggled with something as Coram whispered, "This Yahzed is one of the Scanra gods, I think. A nasty fellow. Dead set against witchcraft, or any magic—"

Alanna frowned. Why had the Goddess sent her this particular vision? What meaning could it have?

Her nostrils caught the scent of burning wood, and someone screamed in agony.

"*Now* you do Yahzed's work!" the priest screamed. "Burn the sorceress! Cleanse this village of her taint!" The people roared their satisfaction; the woman they were burning screamed again.

Alanna reacted. A year ago she would have hesitated; a year ago she had not been a Bazhir shaman. Bolts of purple fire flamed from her open palm, knocking those they touched to the ground. "No!" she screamed. When they turned to charge, she pointed the crystal sword, opening a chasm at their feet.

"Fiend!" the priest cried, holding up a large black star-shaped pendant. A jewel at its middle twinkled in the sun and caught Alanna's eye, but that trick had been played on her once before: Duke Roger had been far cleverer at it than this man. She reached out, putting her lioness shield between her and the priest as she whispered spell-words. The priest shrieked as first his jewel, then the pendant, shuddered and cracked into a thousand pieces in his grip.

Grim-faced, Alanna rode forward, Coram at her back. Faithful stood erect on the saddle before her, back arched, fur erect, hissing with fury. A villager ran yelling at Alanna, swinging a hoe. Coram swung between them on his bay, knocking the man aside with the flat of his broadsword. Several rocks flew by; one struck Alanna on the head. For a moment she reeled sickly. Sheer fury rose up in her, spilling from the crystal sword in a bolt of magic and hurling three of the rock throwers in the air. The villagers broke and ran.

Alanna freed both hands and reached for the clear azure sky. "Goddess!" she cried to her patron. "Give me rain!"

For a moment all of time froze. Then the ember-stone began to pulse in a slow, majestic rhythm as great thunderheads blotted out the sun. There was a deafening crack of thunder, and the rain flooded down, dousing the fire at the stake.

"Thank you, Great Lady," Alanna whispered, feeling the first niggling touches of exhaustion from her use of magic.

The priest, armed with a dagger, launched himself at her: Faithful jumped to meet him and landed on the man's face. The fanatic screamed, trying to dislodge the cat, until Coram ended his cries with a sword thrust.

"Don't waste yerself on the likes of yon," he advised Faithful as the cat disentangled himself from the body.

Reaching the stake, Alanna cut free the woman they had tried to burn. The victim slumped to her knees among the still-smoldering logs, oblivious to her hurts and to the rain.

Coram joined them, pulling the injured woman

into his saddle, cushioning her gently. "We've got to move," he yelled over the thunder. "They'll be back, better armed, I don't doubt."

"You killed the priest!" A young man, armed with a long axe, was advancing on them. "His god will hold us to blame!"

Alanna dismounted and drew the crystal blade. "Get her out of here!" she ordered Coram, settling her shield on her arm once more. The ex-soldier hesitated, and she yelled, "Do what I say! Before the villagers come!"

Frowning, he obeyed. Alanna faced the armed villager. "Don't be a fool," she told him. "I'm a full knight; you won't stand a chance!"

"You lie!" The man charged, holding his axe in a clearly practiced manner. Alanna caught the downswinging axe on her shield, knocking it aside. In the same motion she sliced up from under her shield with the crystal blade. The man jumped back, skidding in the mud, and Alanna hacked the axe blade from its handle. The crystal blade hummed, filling her with the sick killing joy she thought she had wiped from its makeup. Alanna staggered, her vision clouding.

The young man yelled with delight, swinging the axe haft in a blow that connected solidly with Alanna's unprotected right side. She dropped to her knees, just getting the shield up in time as he swung on her head. The crystal sword screamed in her mind, demanding the life of the man who was attacking her. Alanna's hand was sweating, making the hilt slippery in her grasp. *Was this how Akhnan Ibn Nazzir felt when he used his life-force trying to kill me?* she wondered. She threw the sword aside and hurled herself off the ground, ramming the shield at the villager.

He yelled and dropped back, letting the axe haft fall. Alanna swooped and grabbed it. She put herself between the crystal sword and the villager, watching him intently.

"The sword's magic," she panted as he stared at her. "If you take it, it'll kill you. Why would I throw it away, otherwise?'

"I don't believe you," he gasped.

"Then try to get it."

He darted to the side and forward, thinking she would not be fast enough. Alanna brought the axe haft down on his head, knocking him unconscious to the ground.

For a moment she swayed, gathering the strength to kneel and see if she had killed him. His pulse was steady and strong; he had a lump on his head, but she judged he would survive.

"Maybe now you won't go attacking strange knights," she whispered, wiping the sweat from her face. She picked up the crystal sword and resheathed it, feeling no trace of its magic.

"Maybe that was its last try to turn me to breaking and killing," she told Faithful, who had stayed well out of the battle.

Are you willing to bet on that? the cat wanted to know.

Alanna gathered Moonlight's reins and mounted. "Not in the least."

Faithful jumped onto the saddle, and Alanna turned the mare away from the village. She stopped once at the square's edge to look back; the tall post still stood, lit by flickering lightning. Alanna pointed at it and spoke a single powerful word. The stake blasted from the ground as if shot from a bow, shattering into fragments no larger than toothpicks.

Alanna and Coram halted by the marker they had seen that morning. Hurriedly the knight spread a groundcover on the wet grass; Coram gently placed the sorceress on it. The woman they had saved was in her forties, dark-haired, her eyes a deep brown. Old and new bruises covered her; a trickle of fresh blood accented the corner of her mouth. She was badly burned.

Taking her hand, Alanna reached with her Gift, already knowing what she would find.

"Don't spend your strength, child." The woman's voice was hoarse. "I know I am dying."

Alanna withdrew, sick at heart. "How did you get such deep injuries?"

"They stoned me yesterday," was the answer. "My poor children, who will look after them now?"

"Ye're sorry for *them?*" Coram asked, astounded.

"It has been a terrible winter," she whispered.

"The food was running out. Yahzed's priest told them it was because of me: that the foodstores would renew themselves if they had me killed. They were hungry."

"Fools!" Coram muttered.

The sorceress took Alanna's hand. "You two have given me the death I did not hope to have, lying at peace among friends. Halef Seif sent you?" Alanna nodded. "I prayed he could help. Never think you came too late. My life was over when they laid hands on me a week ago. How could I live knowing the ones I had brought into the world and cared for wanted me dead?" Squeezing Alanna's hand, she said, "Open your heart to me."

Alanna felt the sorceress in her mind as a kind, gentle presence easing her bitterness over the woman's impending death. A second later the older female released Alanna's hand, sweating and trembling from her efforts.

"You are the one I need," she gasped. "Listen, Alanna of Trebond! I can give you a gift. Will you accept it?"

Alanna touched the ember-stone. It was warm, but not hot, and she realized what the sorceress had to say was important. "Go on."

The woman's battered lips parted in a smile. "Listen well! You have the knowledge to restore your broken sword: it was in the spell that made you one with the Bloody Hawk and one with your foster-father. It lies in the spell that made the Prince the Voice of the Tribes. Take the crystal sword and make it one with the sword that is your own. You will need it: a dark time is coming for Tortall."

Alanna nodded, biting a trembling lip.

The sorceress reached inside her tattered dress and produced a scorched silk envelope that bulged with its contents. "I would have let this burn, but now you may take it to Halef Seif. He will know what to do." She shuddered, her limbs twitching. When the convulsion passed, she said, "Let nothing stop you from giving that envelope to Halef Seif!"

"I'll do it," Alanna told her. "Don't fret."

The woman nodded. "I'm so tired," she whispered. "Thank you." She smiled at Faithful. "All three of you." Her breathing was suddenly shallow. "Tell Halef I will be waiting when he makes the journey...."

Her voice trailed off. Within moments her breath had stopped, and Alanna gently closed her eyes. Tear-blinded, she stood.

Coram buried the sorceress. "Did ye even know her name?"

Alanna shook her head, watching her companion shovel the last bit of dirt onto the grave. "Halef Seif never mentioned it, and neither did she."

"A pity to leave her without a marker," Coram admitted somberly. "But it's our lives to go to the village and find out."

"She'll have a marker," Alanna whispered.

You don't have the strength, Faithful cautioned. *When will you learn when to stop?*

"I'm going to do this one last thing," she retorted. "Stand back, both of you."

As Coram and Faithful obeyed, she clenched her fists. There was no spell for what she wanted to do, but she was determined not to let that stop her. If the will to accomplish was the greatest part of any magic, she had only to tell the earth what she required, and that was what she did. The ground beyond the head of the grave shook as she pulled at it. When she opened her tightly closed eyes, a granite pillar stood to mark the burying place. Deeply-graven letters proclaimed, "Here lies the sorceress of Alois, who loved the people who killed her."

∽

Coram took over, getting her as far away from the village as possible. She was barely conscious when he chose a campsite. She collapsed exhausted onto the ground, barely waking when Coram tucked her into her bedroll. He couldn't wake her the next morning. Since Faithful showed no signs of alarm, he settled down for a day of relaxation, keeping a watchful eye on his knight-mistress as he whittled.

It was sunset when she awoke, getting away from a dream:

The throne room was filled: the King and Queen on their thrones, Duke Gareth beside the King, Jon with the Queen. Although she could see clearly, she heard no sounds coming from people's mouths. Her friends watched with mingled awe and horror as

Thom introduced a bowing man to his sovereigns.
That man looked around into Alanna's eyes: he was
Roger of Conté. She could hear him clearly as he
remarked, "I don't kill easily, do I, Lioness? But thank
your brother for this. And mind you bring back my
sword."

She sat bolt upright, her clothing damp with
sweat.

"Nightmares again?" Coram asked, stirring a
pot of stew. It was nearly dark. "They're never real,
lass. Have some food."

She told him the dream as they ate. The sight of
their fire and of Faithful playing with wood shav-
ings finally reassured her.

"Sometimes I wonder if I don't *want* him to
come back," she sighed, putting down her bowl.
"But that doesn't make sense, does it?"

Coram blew an experimental note on the flute
he had carved. "Well, the two of ye had some unfin-
ished business," he commented. "And think. It's not
granted to all of us to have one great enemy. The
Duke was yers. The problem is that once ye've van-
quished such an enemy, life might be a little empty.
Ye've spent so much time thinking about him, and
now he's not there to worry ye any more."

"You don't think I'm having—well, prophetic
dreams?"

"Have ye had them before?"

"No. Visions, sometimes, but not dreams."

"It doesn't seem likely ye'd start having them at

such a late date. Yer dreams are still just dreams."
He watched with misgiving as she put the crystal
blade and the two parts of Lightning on the ground
before her. "*Now* what're ye up to?"

"She told me how to mend Lightning, and
that's what I'm going to do."

Faithful came to sit beside her as Coram
backed away. For a moment Alanna stared resent-
fully at the two long scars on her right forearm.
Gritting her teeth, she drew a third wound beside
them with her dagger, letting her blood drip onto
both swords. A harsh wind sprang up; their fire
burned purple.

"One," Alanna whispered, closing her eyes and
fumbling for the best words. "Crystal and whole,
unbreakable, strong. One—crystal in the hilt,
straight steel, sheared in two." Dust whipped
against her face. "Two—" She moved the three
pieces closer to each other. "Separate, yet together.
Being. Becoming." Power shuddered through her
body. "One!" she yelled over the shrieking wind.
"One blade, unbreakable and whole!"

A last flare of power blasted through her,
unbearable in its strength: Alanna fainted.

"Of all the crazy, stupid stunts." Coram's famil-
iar grumble soaked through the darkness around
her. "Ye'd think ye'd wait till ye recovered from the
fireworks yesterday, but not ye." Alanna swam up
out of the dark, toward his voice. "No, ye must
prove ye're Lord Thom and can do anything."

Alanna forced her eyes open, grinning weakly at the man who was propping her up. She was wrapped in her blankets. "I just wanted to fix my sword. No more fireworks tonight, Coram, I promise."

He snorted, clearly disbelieving her. Carefully he picked up something and fitted her hand around the hilt.

She was almost too tired to lift it. Lightning's battered round crystal topped the silver hilt. The blade was thin, as Lightning's had been; it was steel with a ghostly gray sheen. There was no feel of alien magic or anger in it, and the sword fit Alanna's hand well.

As she looked it over, Coram observed, "Ye've traveled a distance, haven't ye? 'Twas only a year ago ye said ye'd never use yer magic again. Now ye're a shaman and makin' up yer own spells."

Alanna smiled ruefully. "Have you ever noticed that when you try to deny some part of yourself, things fall out so you need that part more than any other? I was afraid of magic, partly because I was sure it couldn't be controlled. But the crystal sword taught me it can. Before I came to the Bazhir, I saw a lot of magic used only to harm; being shaman cured me of that. I guess I'm not afraid of my Gift anymore. *I'm* the one who wields it—my Gift doesn't wield me. And now I can help the people I swore to help with my abilities. Does that make any sense?" she asked worriedly.

Coram grinned. "As much sense as anything from the mouth of a noble."

"*You've* been living among thieves too long," Alanna told him. Testing her thumb on the sword's edge, she cut herself. Smiling with delight, she hefted Lightning. "*Now* I'm ready for anything!"

"Speakin' of anything," Coram said as he banked the fire for the night. "What next? Where do we go in the morning?"

Someplace new? Faithful wanted to know. His tail was twitching with excitement.

Alanna crawled into her bedroll, feeling exhausted but satisfied. "Well, we need to take the sorceress's envelope to Halef Seif." She yawned. "It must be pretty important, or she wouldn't have tried to burn it rather than let anyone she didn't trust have it."

"Very well. And then?"

"I think we'll ride south," Alanna told her companions. "King Barnesh of Maren is holding a great tournament in April. I want to start acting like a knight again. And maybe we'll find some adventures along the way. Sound good?"

It's about time, Faithful grumbled as he curled up beside her nose.

From his own bedroll, Coram said, "It sounds beautiful. Now get some rest, Lioness."

Alanna reached beside her and found Lightning's hilt. She gripped her restored blade as she moved toward sleep, a weary smile on her lips.

Her first year as a knight was over. She had survived. And if there was trouble ahead, well, she was
ready for it.

*T*AMORA PIERCE was born in western Pennsylvania in 1954, has lived in various states across America, and currently resides in Manhattan. A graduate of the University of Pennsylvania, she studied social work, film, and psychology. She has been a martial arts movie reviewer, housemother in a group home, a literary agent's assistant, head writer for a radio production company, and an investment banking secretary. She is married to writer/film-maker Tim Liebe. They are owned by two cats (the Lioness, better known as Scrap, and Vinnie) and by Zorak, an attitudinal parakeet.

Ms. Pierce began writing stories when she was eleven. Her published books include the Song of the Lioness quartet (*Alanna: The First Adventure, In the Hand of the Goddess, The Woman Who Rides Like a Man,* and *Lioness Rampant*) and the Immortals quartet (*Wild Magic, Wolf-Speaker, Emperor Mage,* and *The Realms of the Gods*), which have also been translated into German and Danish. Ms. Pierce has already started working on her next series.

*Alanna's legend continues in the final book
in the Song of the Lioness Quartet*

Lioness Rampant

now a Random House Fantasy paperback.

On a March afternoon a knight and a man-at-arms reached the gates of the Marenite city of Berat. The guards hid their smiles as they looked the noble over—in size the beardless youth could as well have been a squire, with only a shield to reveal his higher rank. They wondered aloud if the youngster could *hold* his lance, let alone unseat an opponent with it. Hearing them, the knight favored them with a broad grin. The guards, liking his reaction, fell silent. The man-at-arms gave a tug on their packhorse's lead rein, and the small party moved through the gates into the city.

Most nobles dressed richly, but this knight wore well-traveled leather, covered with a white burnoose like those worn by the Bazhir of the Tortallan desert. With the burnoose's hood pushed back, everyone could see that the knight's hair was copper, cut so it brushed his shoulders. His eyes were an odd, purple shade that drew stares; his face determined. Before him, in a cup fixed to his mare's saddle, rode a black cat.

The man-at-arms was dressed like the knight. There were no grins for him—he was a burly, dark-haired commoner with no-nonsense eyes. It was he who asked directions to the inn called the Wandering Bard while the knight looked with interest at the streets around them. They set off in the direction of the inn, picking their way through the crowds with ease.

The cat swiveled his head, looking up at the knight. *They think you're a boy.* To most, his utterances sounded like those of any cat; to the few he chose, he spoke as plainly as a human.

"Good," the knight replied. "That's less fuss over me."

Is that why you left your shield covered?

"Be sensible, Faithful," was the tart reply. "The shield's covered because I don't want it to get all over dust. It takes forever to clean it. This far south, who'd've heard of *me*?"

The man-at-arms, who'd drawn level with them, grinned. "Ye'd be surprised. News has a way of travelin'."

❧

*T*he common room of the Wandering Bard was deserted except for the innkeeper, Windfeld, who was resting after the noon rush. He'd just begun his own meal when a stable boy charged in.

"Y'want t'hurry, master," the boy puffed, excited. "They's a knight in th'yards—a Tortall knight!"

"What of that?" Windfeld replied. "We've had knights at the Bard afore."

"Not a knight like this'un," the boy announced. "This'un be a *girl!*"

"Don't joke with me, lad," Windfeld began. Then he remembered. "That's right. Sir Myles wrote me of the lass he adopted a year past. Said she went as a lad for years, as page and squire, till she was knighted. That was when our stables almost burned, and I didn't pay his letter the attention I ought. What's her shield?"

"Shield's a-covered" was the reply. "But her man wears a pin like one. It's red, with a gold cat a-rearin' on it."

"That's her—Alanna of Trebond and Olau, Sir Myles's heir." Windfeld got up, removing his apron to throw it on the table. "And with the Shang Dragon here already! It's bound to be a good week. The stableyard, you said?"

❧

*A*lanna of Trebond and Olau, sometimes called "the Lioness" for the cat on her shield, was surprised to be greeted by the innkeeper. The host of such a prosperous house did not meet his guests unless they were wealthy or famous. Since she had lived in Tortall's Great Southern Desert for over a year, Alanna did not realize *she* had become famous.

Afoot, her cat cradled in her arms, she was short and stocky—sturdy rather than muscular. She did not look as if she could have disguised her sex for years to undergo a knight's harsh training. And she certainly did not look as if she would excel at her training to the point where some—men who were qualified to judge such matters—would call her "the finest squire in Tortall."

She also did not look like the adopted heir of one of her realm's wealthiest noblemen. "I don't know if Sir Myles told you," Windfeld explained, "but I'm honored to serve his interests here in Berat. I bid you and your man welcome to the Wanderin' Bard." He nodded to the man-at-arms, who supervised the stabling of the horses. "Whatever you wish, just let my folk know. Would the two of you like a cool drink, to lay the dust?"

"I'll see to the packs and the rooms," the man told them. "I know," he said quickly as his knight-mistress opened her mouth. "Ye're wantin' a bath; hot water, soap, and soon." He grinned at Windfeld. "She's that finicky, for a lass who's livin' on the road."

Alanna shrugged. "What can I say? I like to be clean. Thanks, Coram."

"He's been with you long?" Windfeld asked as he showed her into the common room, indicated a seat, and sat down facing her.

"Forever," Alanna replied. "Coram changed my diapers, and he never lets me forget it. He helped raise my twin brother and me." To a maid who'd come to ask what she'd like, Alanna said, "Fruit juice would be wonderful, if you have it."

The innkeeper smiled as the servant girl left. "The Wanderin' Bard has whatever may hit your fancy, Lady Alanna. How is your honored father, if you don't mind my askin'?"

The maid returned with a pitcher and a tankard on a tray, presenting them to Alanna. Taking a swallow from her tankard, the knight sat back with a sigh. "He was fine when last I heard from him two months ago. Coram and I've been on the road for weeks. I've never been out of Tortall before, so we took our time. Maren doesn't seem much different."

Windfeld grinned. "Nor should it, Tortall and Tusaine and Maren bein' cut from the same cloth. Things change, east of here."

Alanna saw a shadow cross her host's face. "Trouble?"

"Just the sickness that comes on a land now and then," was the reply. "There's war in Sarain the last eighteen months or so. Only a Saren could tell you what started it, or what'll finish it. But there," Windfeld added, seeing a chambermaid at the door. "Your rooms be ready, along with your bath."

The knight picked up her cat, who was playing with Windfeld's apron. "Come on, Faithful," she groaned, settling him over her shoulder. "Let's get clean."

A chill went through the innkeeper as he watched them go. Only now had he seen that the cat's eyes were not a proper shade of amber, green, or grey; they were as purple as Alanna's. Instinctively he made the Sign against Evil.

Read all of
Tamora Pierce's

Song of the Lioness Quartet

available wherever books are sold...
OR
You can send in this coupon
(with check or money order)
and have the books mailed directly to you!

❑   Alanna: The First Adventure
     (0-679-80114-6) $4.99
❑   In the Hand of the Goddess
     (0-679-80111-1) $4.99
❑   The Woman Who Rides Like a Man
     (0-679-80112-X) $4.99
❑   Lioness Rampant
     (0-679-80113-8) $4.99

                Subtotal .... $ _____
                Shipping and handling .... $ 3.00
                Sales tax (where applicable) .. $ _____
                Total amount enclosed .... $ _____

Name _____
Address_____
City _____ State _____ Zip _____

Prices and numbers subject to change without notice. Valid in U.S. only.
All orders subject to availability. Please allow 4 to 6 weeks for delivery.

Make your check or money order (no cash or C.O.D.s)
payable to Random House and mail to:
Bullseye Mail Sales, 400 Hahn Road, Westminster, MD 21157.